Collector's Library

TWELFTH NIGHT;
OR, WHAT YOU WILL

TWELFTH NIGHT;
OR, WHAT YOU
WILL

William Shakespeare

INTRODUCTION BY
ROBERT MIGHALL

Collector's Library

This edition published in 2011 by
Collector's Library
an imprint of CRW Publishing Limited,
69 Gloucester Crescent, London NW1 7EG

ISBN 978 1 907360 14 5

2 4 6 8 10 9 7 5 3 1

Typeset in Great Britain by
Bookcraft Ltd, Stroud, Gloucestershire

Printed and bound in China by Imago

Contents

INTRODUCTION

Twelfth Night is one of Shakespeare's most loved love comedies, a perennial favourite with actors and audiences alike. It was probably written and first performed around 1601–2, in the last years of Elizabeth I's reign, as befits a play about endings. The feast of Twelfth Night marked the very last day of the Christmas season, affording a final burst of merriment and mayhem before normality and workaday necessity returned. Shakespeare's play is not literally set on the 6th of January, but celebrates the ethos of the eponymous feast. An ethos embodied in Sir Toby, belching out defiance at those who would send him to bed before he is ready, or school him in sobriety. It is Twelfth Night, after all; there will be time enough for the cares and responsibilities of the world tomorrow. 'Come, come; I'll go burn some sack; 'tis too late to go to bed now' (II.3.185).

This spirit of carefree hedonism – at least on the play's surface – is infectious, accounting for the enduring popularity of what is easily one of Shakespeare's funniest and most accessible plays. The knockabout, word play and bawdy humour translate effortlessly down the centuries, with a host of grotesques almost defying actors to test the limits of comic excess. But as with pantomime (another cross-dressing, topsy-turvy revel associated with the Christmas season), to go too far in any of these roles would be quite an achievement.

The comic lineup of Belch, Aguecheek and Malvolio dominating the drama is another expression of the Twelfth Night ethos the play enshrines. Twelfth Night traditionally sanctioned the overturning of conventional roles. For one night master might change places with servant, and attend him at the feast. And so it is that the relatively 'minor' characters, to which must be added Feste the fool, and Maria the serving woman, rule our affections, lording it over those who appear first in the Dramatis Personae and the social hierarchy. Whilst there have been few really memorable Count Orsinos, major actors at the height of their careers have clamoured to give their definitive Sir Toby (Sir Laurence Olivier: Ralph Richardson; Malvolio (Alec Guiness; Anthony Sher; Nigel Hawthorne); or Feste (Ben Kingsley). The fun is to be had in the servant's quarters, rather than in the state rooms, where their 'betters' are too busy moping over unrequited love or mourning dead relatives to delight us much. As Sir Toby states in this opening address: 'What a plague means my niece, to take the death of her brother thus? I am sure care's an enemy to life'. (I, 3, 1). Twelfth Night is no occasion for mourning.

Such role reversals are central to the drama, where the topsy turvy ethos of the feast is played out on a number of levels. The most obvious level is the sexual, where masters and servants change roles for a while. A girl disguised as a serving boy falls in love with her master and can only declare her love through (nearly transparent) riddles. The master is so caught up in believing and professing himself in love with a Countess he fails to decipher them. He only has eyes and high-flown romantic rhetoric for Olivia. She, despite their social suitability, rejects his suit. Orsino makes Viola / Cesario his 'favourite', and enlists him as erotic envoy in his campaign against Olivia's indifference. 'Cesario' is tasked with using his eloquence in the language of love to win Olivia over, a language steeped in Courtly poetic conventions, where to love is to 'serve' or be enslaved by a mistress.

But the eloquence works too well, or rather too literally, when Olivia falls head over heels (how often love is depicted as a revolution) for this young 'servant'. She is prepared to overturn social hierarchy by the power of sexual desire. Yet another reversal of roles. From being the indifferent object of another's unrequited desire, she is swiftly dealt a dose of her own medicine in her helpless, hopeless passion for a decidedly unsuitable sexual object. The social rules are suspended while a countess is in love with and prepared to marry a servant. To say nothing of the sexual rules or conventions given the fact that the servant is actually a woman.

The plays thus dallies with homoerotic potentialities, which modern directors and commentators have been more than ready to explore or exploit to the full. The love of Olivia for Viola, in the guise of Cesario, and, in part, Orsino for his effeminate favourite (whom he marries with such swiftness once her true gender is revealed that one is compelled to speculate on 'Cesario's' role as a warm up act), are mirrored in more overt form by Antonio's professed love for Sebastian. This is as charged with the language of devotion and 'service' as fully as the play's heterosexual exchanges: 'My willing love .. set forth in your pursuit' (III, 3, 11). This is the world of Shakespeare's Sonnets brought to dramatic life, where the poet professes a jealous love for a fickle young man, and you make of this What you Will. Disguise might very well be a 'wickedness' as Viola asserts, on realising she has unwittingly seduced a woman; yet it is also a fruitful device for exploring the rules and rhetoric of sexual conventions, or a potent weapon in the age old war of the sexes.

> We men may say more, swear more: but indeed,
> Our shows are more than will; for still we prove
> Much in our vows, but little in our love. (II, 4, 116–18).

The cross dresser crosses knowledge as well as gender borders. A spy in the house of love, he/she is able to see love from the other side of the sexual divide. So Viola's womanly knowledge affords her an insider's advantage in winning the heart of Olivia; and her disguise as a boy allows her to criticise the hollowness of male courtship by delivering some home truths to Orsino and the mostly male audience at Shakespeare's first performance. This satirical perspective is given further scope in performance, with Viola's often parodying rather than attempting to mimic maleness in their disguised scenes.

Disguise plays a key role in *Twelfth Night*, which is only partly a comedy of errors, as the dramatic possibilities presented by the twins are only exploited fully in the last act

ix

and a half. The arrival of Sebastian into a highly-charged erotic conundrum allows a bit of comic play with the duel scene; but its principal role is to dispel rather than heighten the confusion upon which comedy thrives. It is Act 4, scene 2, so his role is a *deus ex machina* for Cupid's designs – allowing the course of love to flow more smoothly and conventionally with the final abandonment of disguise.

As the setting right of the final act confirms, the anarchy of the Twelfth Night topsy turvy world is only a temporary license, a sanctioned episode of carnivalesque before social and sexual norms reassert themselves. The play only flirts with anarchy. Servants turn out to be nobly born, and a man arrives in the, aesthetically similar but anatomically distinct, shape of Sebastian to redirect Olivia's errant sexual desire. All's well that ends well in true Shakespearian comic style. Malvolio's conceited ambition to marry his mistress would appear to be a social violation too far. And so he is hoist by his own cross garters in a trap set by his own vanity. Malvolio's bid to overturn social distinctions by marrying his noble mistress is of a different order to the disguised disruption threatened by Olivia's love for a 'servant'. His comic punishment is again in the spirit of the feast, bringing low a puffed up figure of authority who abuses his office. As Sir Toby challenges him: 'Art any more than a steward?' (II, 3, 111). A prime target for toppling on a night of licensed misrule.

And a very English comic character dealt a suitably English comic comeuppance. Pomposity might be considered an English vice, nurtured by the rigidly stratified, class-obsessed society that still prevails. Malvolio gets 'above himself', and so is cut down to size through a ridicule that is the stock-in-trade of situation comedy even today. Even a comedy that celebrates the temporary breach of social distinctions and decorums cannot countenance a conceited upstart, and so Malvolio is dealt a severe form of justice by Toby, Maria and Feste, the characters with whom we most closely identify. We exult and collude in this revenge comedy. Yet Malvolio is also a kind of Puritan, so the comedy would have had a precise relevance for Shakespeare's first audience – indeed, even up to Dickens's day, where the stern, non-conformist, fanatical killjoy remained a stock satirical target. Such figures are often hypocrites, as Malvolio is also revealed to be. For he is only a 'kind' of Puritan, and is more than ready to eschew the sober black of his brethren for vain sartorial fopperies when it believes it will gain him advantage, or to fantasise about the velvet finery he will adopt when he becomes Count Malvolio, the cosset lover of the fair Olivia. The yellow stockings reveal his true colours, so we applaud the aptness of a vengeance justly visited.

And yet Malvolio is also an outsider, a loner upon whom a 'pack' of bullies in buskins mercilessly gang up. So whilst the English can't abide an upstart, they also tend to side with the underdog, and make a sacred principle of 'fair play'. The foolery is taken too far, and from being a figure of ridicule the much-abused steward becomes an object of pathos. Sir Toby and Andrew Aguecheek are in turn punished for their cruelty by the injuries they sustain from the duel. The characterization and handling of Malvolio straddles the English ethical spectrum, allowing for a shift in sympathies to take place in even the giddiest Twelfth Night audience. Such complexity is of course the hallmark of Shakespeare's genius. 'A sentence is but a cheveril glove to good wit', as Feste claims, 'how quickly the wrong side may be turn'd outward' (III, 1, 11). A character may be turned similarly by a dextrous dramatist, with our sympathies duly following.

The potential pathos residing in the comic grotesque Malvolio, points to a darker thread interwoven through the gilded fabric of Shakespeare's comedy. It can't all be cakes and ale, even on Twelfth Night. In this respect, *Twelfth Night* might be partly compared with such problem comedies as *Measure for Measure* or *The Merchant of Venice* which characterise Shakespeare's maturity. With them 'comedy' is almost wholly a generic designation, premised largely on the fact that the plays end happily. For some that is.

Malvolio, like Shylock in *Merchant*, is marginalised, upon whom a revenge is enacted according to the play's moral code, and who exits the play calling for a further allocation of justice: 'I'll be revenged on the whole pack of you!' If this were Hollywood, we might anticipate a sequel – *The 13th Day: The Revenge of the Puritans*, perhaps – which in some ways came to pass when in 1642 the Puritan faction enforced the closing of the London theatres. 'Virtue' finally triumphing over cakes and ale (at least until the Restoration), and Malvolio having the last laugh after all.

Yet *Twelfth Night* is not tragedy tortured into comedy as it is with *Measure for Measure*. The darker strain in *Twelfth Night* might be considered more in terms of 'tragic relief', the counterpart of the gallows humour which lightens the tragic load that *Hamlet* lays upon the human heart. But a few clouds momentarily obscure the May-morning merriment the play celebrates. Even the complete oaf, Andrew Aguecheek is afforded a measure of pathos that arrests us in our mirth when he sighs plaintively 'I was adored once too' (II, 3, 176). Tragi-comedy, comic-tragedy is the hallmark of Shakespearean greatness. His drama is mixed because life is too.

We might even see Malvolio and Hamlet as being cut from the same cloth. The black-clad tragic misanthrope has his moments of killjoy puritanism – complaining of the heavy-drinking and late hours of the Danish court – as much as the comic stooge Malvolio can elicit tragic pathos when he appears before us caged, friendless, persecuted. Genre largely dictates whether we feel with or laugh at these characters. If the mind of Orsino is an 'opal' – changeable under different lights – it is perhaps because his creator's was too, displaying the complexity of his art through the variegated richness of his characterisation.

This richness extends even to the music of this most musical of Shakespeare's plays. Ostensibly part of the festive spirit Shakespeare's play enshrines, it is not untouched by the melancholy that everywhere intrudes on the revels. Like a skeleton attending a feast, the songs that mark the occasion dwell obsessively on death, time and the brevity of life. Youth's a stuff will not endure. Nor pleasure neither. As John Keats put it in his 'Ode on Melancholy',

> Ay, in the very temple of delight
> Veiled melancholy has her sovran shrine,
> Though seen by none save him whose strenuous tongue
> Can burst joy's grape against his palate fine;

As pleasure turns to poison 'as the bee mouth sips', so the Duke experiences saiety in the song that had just then given him such pleasure, its dying fall initiating the melancholy refrain that recurs throughout the Twelfth Night revels.

For *Twelfth Night* is a play about limits as much about their transgression, drawing the line that divides feast day from the everyday. A feast is temporary, it defies time, but also reinforces its inexorable rule. Especially this feast which marked the end of the Christmas season. Time is triumphant in the end. And so the clock upbraids Olivia, and the final song encompasses the whole of life in a catch. The play's final words reminding us of that most fearful reality: 'every day'.

The play's alternative title, 'Or what you will', makes a virtue of ambiguity. It could suggest license – do as you please -; or encourage multiple perspectives on the tragi-comic fabric of life. This ambiguity has offered rich possibilities for dramatic adaptation down the centuries, commanding some landmark stage performances. And yet whilst the theatre has witnessed an array of A-listers forsaking their preferred tragic roles to try their mettle at Shakespeare's great comic exception, the cinema has largely held back. Trevor Nunn's 1996 adaptation stands out a mile, assembling a cast of seasoned comic actors, including Nigel Hawthorne as a toupéed Malvolio; Richard E Grant as Sir Toby's flaxen-haired gull; and Mel Smith as the merry man himself. The presiding genius of Shakespeare's dark comedy is embodied in a suitably brooding Feste, played by Ben Kingsley, an actor more famous for the dignity or jaggedness of his serious performances. Nunn's autumnal setting and plaintive musical arrangements, bring out perfectly the melancholy at the very heart of this, Shakespeare's most festive revel.

MALVOLIO I will smile; I will do every thing that thou wilt have me.

TWELFTH NIGHT; OR, WHAT YOU WILL

DRAMATIS PERSONAE

ORSINO, *Duke of Illyria.*
SEBASTIAN, *a young gentleman.*
ANTONIO, *a sea captain, friend to Sebastian.*
A SEA CAPTAIN, *friend to Viola.*
VALENTINE, } *gentlemen attending on the Duke.*
CURIO,
SIR TOBY BELCH, *uncle to Olivia.*
SIR ANDREW AGUECHEEK.
MALVOLIO, *steward to Olivia.*
FABIAN, } *servants to Olivia.*
CLOWN,

OLIVIA.
VIOLA, *sister to Sebastian.*
MARIA, *Olivia's woman.*

LORDS, *a* PRIEST, SAILORS, OFFICERS,
MUSICIANS, *and* ATTENDANTS.

SCENE — *A city in Illyria, and the sea-coast near it.*

ACT I

SCENE I

The DUKE'S *palace.*

Enter DUKE, LORDS, *and* CURIO;
MUSICIANS *attending.*

DUKE

If music be the food of love, play on;
Give me excess of it, that, surfeiting,
The appetite may sicken, and so die. —
That strain again! — it had a dying fall:

O, it came o'er my ear like the sweet sound,
That breathes upon a bank of violets,
Stealing and giving odour! — Enough; no more;
'Tis not so sweet now as it was before.
O spirit of love, how quick and fresh art thou!
That, notwithstanding thy capacity
Receiveth as the sea, naught enters there,
Of what validity and pitch soe'er,
But falls into abatement and low price,
Even in a minute! so full of shapes is fancy,
That it alone is high-fantastical.

CURIO

Will you go hunt, my lord?

DUKE

                What, Curio?

CURIO

The hart.

DUKE

Why, so I do, the noblest that I have:
O, when mine eyes did see Olivia first,
Methought she purg'd the air of pestilence!
That instant was I turn'd into a hart;
And my desires, like fell and cruel hounds,
E'er since pursue me.

Enter VALENTINE.

                How now! what news from her?

VALENTINE

So please my lord, I might not be admitted;
But from her handmaid do return this answer:
The element itself, till seven years hence,
Shall not behold her face at ample view;
But, like a cloistress, she will veiled walk,
And water once a day her chamber round
With eye-offending brine: all this to season
A brother's dead love, which she would keep fresh
And lasting in her sad remembrance.

DUKE
O, she that hath a heart of that fine frame
To pay this debt of love but to a brother,
How will she love, when the rich golden shaft
Hath kill'd the flock of all affections else
That live in her; when liver, brain, and heart,
These sovereign thrones, are all supplied, and fill'd
Her sweet perfections with one self king! —
Away before me to sweet beds of flowers:
Love-thoughts lie rich when canopied with bowers.

[*Exeunt.*

SCENE II

The sea-coast.

Enter VIOLA, CAPTAIN, *and* SAILORS.

VIOLA
What country, friends, is this?

CAPTAIN
This is Illyria, lady.

VIOLA
And what should I do in Illyria?
My brother he is in Elysium.
Perchance he is not drown'd: — what think you, sailors?

CAPTAIN
It is perchance that you yourself were saved.

VIOLA
O my poor brother! and so perchance may he be.

CAPTAIN
True, madam; and, to comfort you with chance,
Assure yourself, after our ship did split,
When you, and those poor number sav'd with you,
Hung on our driving boat, I saw your brother,
Most provident in peril, bind himself —
Courage and hope both teaching him the practice —
To a strong mast that liv'd upon the sea;
Where, like Arion on the dolphin's back,

4

I saw him hold acquaintance with the waves
So long as I could see.

VIOLA

For saying so, there's gold:
Mine own escape unfoldeth to my hope,
Whereto thy speech serves for authority,
The like of him. Know'st thou this country?

CAPTAIN

Ay, madam, well; for I was bred and born
Not three hours' travel from this very place.

VIOLA

Who governs here?

CAPTAIN

A noble duke, in nature as in name.

VIOLA

What is his name?

CAPTAIN

Orsino.

VIOLA

Orsino! I have heard my father name him:
He was a bachelor then.

CAPTAIN

And so is now, or was so very late;
For but a month ago I went from hence,
And then 'twas fresh in murmur, — as, you know,
What great ones do, the less will prattle of, —
That he did seek the love of fair Olivia.

VIOLA

What's she?

CAPTAIN

A virtuous maid, the daughter of a count
That died some twelvemonth since; then leaving her
In the protection of his son, her brother,
Who shortly also died: for whose dear loss,
They say, she hath abjur'd the company
And sight of men.

VIOLA

     O, that I serv'd that lady,
And might not be deliver'd to the world,
Till I had made mine own occasion mellow,
What my estate is!

CAPTAIN

     That were hard to compass;
Because she will admit no kind of suit,
No, not the duke's.

VIOLA

There is a fair behaviour in thee, captain;
And though that nature with a beauteous wall
Doth oft close in pollution, yet of thee
I will believe thou hast a mind that suits
With this thy fair and outward character.
I prithee, — and I'll pay thee bounteously, —
Conceal me what I am; and be my aid
For such disguise as haply shall become
The form of my intent. I'll serve this duke:
Thou shalt present me as an eunuch to him:
It may be worth thy pains; for I can sing,
And speak to him in many sorts of music,
That will allow me very worth his service.
What else may hap, to time I will commit;
Only shape thou thy silence to my wit.

CAPTAIN

Be you his eunuch, and your mute I'll be:
When my tongue blabs, then let mine eyes not see.

VIOLA

I thank thee: lead me on.   [*Exeunt.*

SCENE III

Olivia's house.

Enter SIR TOBY BELCH *and* MARIA.

SIR TOBY

What a plague means my niece, to take the death of her
brother thus? I am sure care's an enemy to life.

MARIA

By my troth, Sir Toby, you must come in earlier o'nights: your cousin, my lady, takes great exceptions to your ill hours.

SIR TOBY

Why, let her except before excepted.

MARIA

Ay, but you must confine yourself within the modest limits of order.

SIR TOBY

Confine! I'll confine myself no finer than I am: these clothes are good enough to drink in; and so be these boots too, — an they be not, let them hang themselves in their own straps.

MARIA

That quaffing and drinking will undo you: I heard my lady talk of it yesterday; and of a foolish knight that you brought in one night here to be her wooer.

SIR TOBY I am sure care's an enemy to life.

SIR TOBY
Who, Sir Andrew Aguecheek?

MARIA
Ay, he.

SIR TOBY
He's as tall a man as any's in Illyria.

MARIA
What's that to th'purpose?

SIR TOBY
Why, he has three thousand ducats a year.

MARIA
Ay, but he'll have but a year in all these ducats: he's a very fool and a prodigal.

SIR TOBY
Fie, that you'll say so! he plays o'th'viol-de-gamboys, and speaks three or four languages word for word without book, and hath all the good gifts of nature.

MARIA
He hath, indeed, almost natural: for, besides that he's a fool, he's a great quarreller; and, but that he hath the gift of a coward to allay the gust he hath in quarrelling, 'tis thought among the prudent he would quickly have the gift of a grave.

SIR TOBY
By this hand, they are scoundrels and substractors that say so of him. Who are they?

MARIA
They that add, moreover, he's drunk nightly in your company.

SIR TOBY
With drinking healths to my niece: I'll drink to her as long as there is a passage in my throat and drink in Illyria: he's a coward and a coistrel that will not drink to my niece till his brains turn o'th'toe like a parish-top. What, wench! *Castiliano volto*; for here comes Sir Andrew Agueface.

Enter SIR ANDREW AGUECHEEK.

SIR ANDREW
Sir Toby Belch, — how now, Sir Toby Belch!

SIR TOBY
Sweet Sir Andrew!

SIR ANDREW
Bless you, fair shrew.

MARIA
And you too, sir.

SIR TOBY
Accost, Sir Andrew, accost.

SIR ANDREW
What's that?

SIR TOBY
My niece's chambermaid.

SIR ANDREW
Good Mistress Accost, I desire better acquaintance.

MARIA
My name is Mary, sir.

SIR ANDREW
Good Mistress Mary Accost, —

SIR TOBY
You mistake, knight: 'accost'is front her, board her, woo
her, assail her.

SIR ANDREW
By my troth, I would not undertake her in this
company. Is that the meaning of 'accost'?

MARIA
Fare you well, gentlemen.

SIR TOBY
An thou let part so, Sir Andrew, would thou mightst
never draw sword again.

SIR ANDREW
An you part so, mistress, I would I might never draw sword
again. Fair lady, do you think you have fools in hand?

SIR ANDREW Fair lady, do you think you have fools in hand?.

MARIA
  Sir, I have not you by th'hand.

SIR ANDREW
  Marry, but you shall have; and here's my hand.

MARIA
  Now, sir, thought is free: I pray you, bring your hand to
  th'buttery-bar, and let it drink.

SIR ANDREW
  Wherefore, sweet-heart? what's your metaphor?

MARIA
  It's dry, sir.

SIR ANDREW
  Why, I think so: I am not such an ass but I can keep my
  hand dry. But what's your jest?

MARIA
  A dry jest, sir.

SIR ANDREW
  Are you full of them?

MARIA

Ay, sir, I have them at my fingers' ends: marry, now I let
go your hand, I am barren. [*Exit.*

SIR TOBY

O knight, thou lack'st a cup of canary: when did I see
thee so put down?

SIR ANDREW

Never in your life, I think; unless you see canary put
me down. Methinks sometimes I have no more wit
than a Christian or an ordinary man has: but I am a
great eater of beef, and I believe that does harm to
my wit.

SIR TOBY

No question.

SIR ANDREW

An I thought that, I'ld forswear it. I'll ride home to-
morrow, Sir Toby.

SIR TOBY

Pourquoi, my dear knight?

SIR ANDREW

What is *pourquoi*? do or not do? I would I had bestow'd
that time in the tongues that I have in fencing, dancing,
and bear-baiting: O, had I but follow'd the arts!

SIR TOBY

Then hadst thou had an excellent head of hair.

SIR ANDREW

Why, would that have mended my hair?

SIR TOBY

Past question; for thou seest it will not curl by nature.

SIR ANDREW

But it becomes me well enough, does't not?

SIR TOBY

Excellent; it hangs like flax on a distaff; and I hope to
see a housewife take thee between her legs and spin
it off.

SIR ANDREW

Faith, I'll home to-morrow, Sir Toby: your niece will
not be seen; or if she be, it's four to one she'll none of
me: the count himself here hard by woos her.

SIR TOBY

She'll none o'th'count: she'll not match above her
degree, neither in estate, years, nor wit; I have heard her
swear't. Tut, there's life in't, man.

SIR ANDREW

I'll stay a month longer. I am a fellow o'th'strangest
mind i'th'world; I delight in masks and revels sometimes
altogether.

SIR TOBY

Art thou good at these kickshawses, knight?

SIR ANDREW

As any man in Illyria, whatsoever he be, under the degree
of my betters; and yet I will not compare with a nobleman.

SIR TOBY

What is thy excellence in a galliard, knight?

SIR ANDREW

Faith, I can cut a caper.

SIR TOBY

And I can cut the mutton to't.

SIR ANDREW

And I think I have the back-trick simply as strong as any
man in Illyria.

SIR TOBY

Wherefore are these things hid? wherefore have these
gifts a curtain before 'em? are they like to take dust,
like Mistress Mall's picture? why dost thou not go to
church in a galliard, and come home in a coranto? My
very walk should be a jig; I would not so much as
make water but in a sink-a-pace. What dost thou
mean? is it a world to hide virtues in? I did think, by
the excellent constitution of thy leg, it was form'd
under the star of a galliard.

SIR ANDREW

Ay, 'tis strong, and it does indifferent well in a flame-
colour'd stock. Shall we set about some revels?

SIR TOBY

What shall we do else? were we not born under Taurus?

SIR ANDREW

Taurus! that's sides and heart.

SIR TOBY

No, sir; it is legs and thighs. Let me see thee caper [SIR
ANDREW *dances*]: ha! higher: ha, ha! excellent!

[*Exeunt.*

SCENE IV

The Duke's palace.

Enter VALENTINE, *and* VIOLA *in man's attire.*

VALENTINE

If the duke continue these favours towards you, Cesario,
you are like to be much advanced: he hath known you
but three days, and already you are no stranger.

VIOLA

You either fear his humour or my negligence, that you
call in question the continuance of his love: is he
inconstant, sir, in his favours?

VALENTINE

No, believe me.

VIOLA

I thank you. Here comes the count.

Enter DUKE, CURIO, *and* ATTENDANTS.

DUKE

Who saw Cesario, ho?

VIOLA

On your attendance, my lord; here.

DUKE

Stand you awhile aloof. — Cesario,
Thou know'st no less but all; I have unclasp'd

To thee the book even of my secret soul:
Therefore, good youth, address thy gait unto her,
Be not denied access, stand at her doors,
And tell them, there thy fixed foot shall grow
Till thou have audience.

VIOLA

                Sure, my noble lord,
If she be so abandon'd to her sorrow
As it is spoke, she never will admit me.

DUKE

Be clamorous, and leap all civil bounds,
Rather than make unprofited return.

VIOLA

Say I do speak with her, my lord, what then?

DUKE

O, then unfold the passion of my love,
Surprise her with discourse of my dear faith!
It shall become thee well to act my woes;
She will attend it better in thy youth
Than in a nuncio of more grave aspect.

VIOLA

I think not so, my lord.

DUKE

                Dear lad, believe it;
For they shall yet belie thy happy years,
That say thou art a man: Diana's lip
Is not more smooth and rubious; thy small pipe
Is as the maiden's organ, shrill and sound;
And all is semblative a woman's part.
I know thy constellation is right apt
For this affair: — some four or five attend him;
All, if you will; for I myself am best
When least in company: — prosper well in this,
And thou shalt live as freely as thy lord,
To call his fortunes thine.

VIOLA

                I'll do my best

To woo your lady: — [*aside*] yet, a barful strife!
Whoe'er I woo, myself would be his wife.   [*Exeunt.*

SCENE V

OLIVIA'S *house.*

Enter MARIA *and* CLOWN.

MARIA

Nay, either tell me where thou hast been, or I will not
open my lips so wide as a bristle may enter in way of thy
excuse: my lady will hang thee for thy absence.

CLOWN

Let her hang me: he that is well hang'd in this world
needs to fear no colours.

MARIA

Make that good.

CLOWN

He shall see none to fear.

MARIA

A good lenten answer: I can tell thee where that saying
was born, of, — I fear no colours.

CLOWN

Where, good Mistress Mary?

MARIA

In the wars; and that may you be bold to say in your
foolery.

CLOWN

Well, God give them wisdom that have it; and those that
are fools, let them use their talents.

MARIA

Yet you will be hang'd for being so long absent; or, to be
turn'd away, — is not that as good as a hanging to you?

CLOWN

Many a good hanging prevents a bad marriage; and, for
turning away, let summer bear it out.

MARIA

You are resolute, then?

CLOWN

Not so, neither; but I am resolved on two points.

MARIA

That if one break, the other will hold; or, if both break,
your gaskins fall.

CLOWN

Apt, in good faith; very apt. Well, go thy way; if Sir
Toby would leave drinking, thou wert as witty a piece of
Eve's flesh as any in Illyria.

MARIA

Peace, you rogue, no more o' that. Here comes my lady:
make your excuse wisely, you were best.   [*Exit.*

CLOWN

Wit, an't be thy will, put me into good fooling! Those
wits, that think they have thee, do very oft prove fools;
and I, that am sure I lack thee, may pass for a wise man:
for what says Quinapalus? 'Better a witty fool than a
foolish wit.'

     Enter LADY OLIVIA *with* MALVOLIO.

God bless thee, lady!

OLIVIA

Take the fool away.

CLOWN

Do you not hear, fellows? Take away the lady.

OLIVIA

Go to, y'are a dry fool: I'll no more of you: besides, you
grow dishonest.

CLOWN

Two faults, madonna, that drink and good counsel will
amend: for give the dry fool drink, then is the fool not
dry: bid the dishonest man mend himself; if he mend, he
is no longer dishonest: if he cannot, let the botcher
mend him: any thing that's mended is but patch'd:
virtue that transgresses is but patch'd with sin; and sin

that amends is but patch'd with virtue: if that this simple
syllogism will serve, so; if it will not, what remedy? As
there is no true cuckold but calamity, so beauty's a
flower. — The lady bade take away the fool; therefore, I
say again, take her away.

OLIVIA

Sir, I bade them take away you.

CLOWN

Misprision in the highest degree! — Lady, *cucullus non
facit monachum*; that's as much to say as, I wear not
motley in my brain. Good madonna, give me leave to
prove you a fool.

OLIVIA

Can you do it?

CLOWN

Dexteriously, good madonna.

OLIVIA

Make your proof.

CLOWN

I must catechise you for it, madonna: good my mouse of
virtue, answer me.

OLIVIA

Well, sir, for want of other idleness, I'll bide your proof.

CLOWN

Good madonna, why mourn'st thou?

OLIVIA

Good fool, for my brother's death.

CLOWN

I think his soul is in hell, madonna.

OLIVIA

I know his soul is in heaven, fool.

CLOWN

The more fool, madonna, to mourn for your brother's
soul being in heaven. — Take away the fool,
gentlemen.

OLIVIA

What think you of this fool, Malvolio? doth he not
mend?

MALVOLIO

Yes, and shall do till the pangs of death shake him:
infirmity, that decays the wise, doth ever make the better
fool.

CLOWN

God send you, sir, a speedy infirmity, for the better
increasing your folly! Sir Toby will be sworn that I am
no fox; but he will not pass his word for twopence that
you are no fool.

OLIVIA

How say you to that, Malvolio?

MALVOLIO

I marvel your ladyship takes delight in such a barren
rascal: I saw him put down the other day with an
ordinary fool, that has no more brain than a stone. Look
you now, he's out of his guard already; unless you laugh
and minister occasion to him, he is gagg'd. I protest, I
take these wise men, that crow so at these set kind of
fools, no better than the fools' zanies.

OLIVIA

O, you are sick of self-love, Malvolio, and taste with a
distemper'd appetite. To be generous, guiltless, and of
free disposition, is to take those things for bird-bolts that
you deem cannon-bullets: there is no slander in an
allow'd fool, though he do nothing but rail; nor no
railing in a known discreet man, though he do nothing
but reprove.

CLOWN

Now Mercury endue thee with leasing, for thou speak'st
well of fools!

Enter MARIA.

MARIA

Madam, there is at the gate a young gentleman much desires to speak with you.

OLIVIA

From the Count Orsino, is it?

MARIA

I know not, madam: 'tis a fair young man, and well attended.

OLIVIA

Who of my people hold him in delay?

MARIA

Sir Toby, madam, your kinsman.

OLIVIA

Fetch him off, I pray you; he speaks nothing but madman: fie on him! [*Exit* MARIA.] Go you, Malvolio: if it be a suit from the count, I am sick, or not at home; what you will, to dismiss it. [*Exit* MALVOLIO.] Now you see, sir, how your fooling grows old, and people dislike it.

CLOWN

Thou hast spoke for us, madonna, as if thy eldest son should be a fool; whose skull Jove cram with brains! for — here he comes — one of thy kin has a most weak *pia mater*.

Enter SIR TOBY.

OLIVIA

By mine honour, half drunk. — What is he at the gate, cousin?

SIR TOBY

A gentleman.

OLIVIA

A gentleman! what gentleman?

SIR TOBY

'Tis a gentleman here — a plague o' these pickle-herring! — How now, sot!

CLOWN

Good Sir Toby! —

OLIVIA

Cousin, cousin, how have you come so early by this
lethargy?

SIR TOBY

Lechery! I defy lechery. There's one at the gate.

OLIVIA

Ay, marry, what is he?

SIR TOBY

Let him be the devil, an he will, I care not: give me faith,
say I. Well, it's all one. [*Exit.*

OLIVIA

What's a drunken man like, fool?

CLOWN

Like a drown'd man, a fool, and a madman: one
draught above heat makes him a fool; the second mads
him; and a third drowns him.

OLIVIA

Go thou and seek the crowner, and let him sit o' my
coz; for he's in the third degree of drink, — he's
drown'd: go, look after him.

CLOWN

He is but mad yet, madonna; and the fool shall look to the
madman. [*Exit.*

Enter MALVOLIO.

MALVOLIO

Madam, yond young fellow swears he will speak with
you. I told him you were sick; he takes on him to
understand so much, and therefore comes to speak with
you: I told him you were asleep; he seems to have a
foreknowledge of that too, and therefore comes to speak
with you. What is to be said to him, lady? he's fortified
against any denial.

OLIVIA

Tell him he shall not speak with me.

MALVOLIO

Has been told so; and he says, he'll stand at your door
like a sheriff's post, and be the supporter to a bench, but
he'll speak with you.

OLIVIA

What kind o' man is he?

MALVOLIO

Why, of mankind.

OLIVIA

What manner of man?

MALVOLIO

Of very ill manner; he'll speak with you, will you or no.

OLIVIA

Of what personage and years is he?

MALVOLIO

Not yet old enough for a man, nor young enough for a
boy; as a squash is before 'tis a peascod, or a codling
when 'tis almost an apple: 'tis with him e'en standing
water, between boy and man. He is very well-favour'd,
and he speaks very shrewishly; one would think his
mother's milk were scarce out of him.

OLIVIA

Let him approach: call in my gentlewoman.

MALVOLIO

Gentlewoman, my lady calls. [*Exit.*

Enter MARIA.

OLIVIA

Give me my veil: come, throw it o'er my face.
We'll once more hear Orsino's embassy.

Enter VIOLA.

VIOLA

The honourable lady of the house, which is she?

OLIVIA

Speak to me; I shall answer for her. Your will?

VIOLA

Most radiant, exquisite, and unmatchable beauty, — I pray you, tell me if this be the lady of the house, for I never saw her: I would be loth to cast away my speech; for, besides that it is excellently well penn'd, I have taken great pains to con it. Good beauties, let me sustain no scorn; I am very comptible, even to the least sinister usage.

OLIVIA

Whence came you, sir?

VIOLA

I can say little more than I have studied, and that question's out of my part. Good gentle one, give me modest assurance if you be the lady of the house, that I may proceed in my speech.

OLIVIA

Are you a comedian?

VIOLA

No, my profound heart: and yet, by the very fangs of malice I swear I am not that I play. Are you the lady of the house?

OLIVIA

If I do not usurp myself, I am.

VIOLA

Most certain, if you are she, you do usurp yourself; for, what is yours to bestow is not yours to reserve. But this is from my commission: I will on with my speech in your praise, and then show you the heart of my message.

OLIVIA

Come to what is important in't: I forgive you the praise.

VIOLA

Alas, I took great pains to study it, and 'tis poetical.

OLIVIA

It is the more like to be feign'd: I pray you, keep it in. I heard you were saucy at my gates; and allow'd your approach rather to wonder at you than to hear you. If

22

you be mad, be gone; if you have reason, be brief: 'tis
not that time of moon with me to make one in so
skipping a dialogue.

MARIA

Will you hoist sail, sir? here lies your way.

VIOLA

No, good swabber; I am to hull here a little longer.
Some mollification for your giant, sweet lady. Tell me
your mind: I am a messenger.

OLIVIA

Sure, you have some hideous matter to deliver, when the
courtesy of it is so fearful. Speak your office.

VIOLA

It alone concerns your ear. I bring no overture of war,
no taxation of homage: I hold the olive in my hand; my
words are as full of peace as matter.

OLIVIA

Yet you began rudely. What are you? what would you?

VIOLA

The rudeness that hath appear'd in me have I learn'd
from my entertainment. What I am, and what I would,
are as secret as maidenhead: to your ears, divinity; to
any other's, profanation.

OLIVIA

Give us the place alone: we will hear this divinity.
[*Exit* MARIA.] Now, sir, what is your text?

VIOLA

Most sweet lady, —

OLIVIA

A comfortable doctrine, and much may be said of it.
Where lies your text?

VIOLA

In Orsino's bosom.

OLIVIA

In his bosom! In what chapter of his bosom?

23

VIOLA

To answer by the method, in the first of his heart.

OLIVIA

O, I have read it: it is heresy. Have you no more to say?

VIOLA

Good madam, let me see your face.

OLIVIA

Have you any commission from your lord to negotiate
with my face? You are now out of your text: but we will
draw the curtain, and show you the picture. Look you,
sir, such a one I was, this presents: is't not well done?

[*Unveiling.*

VIOLA

Excellently done, if God did all.

OLIVIA

'Tis in grain, sir; 'twill endure wind and weather.

VIOLA

'Tis beauty truly blent, whose red and white
Nature's own sweet and cunning hand laid on:
Lady, you are the cruell'st she alive,
If you will lead these graces to the grave,
And leave the world no copy.

OLIVIA

O, sir, I will not be so hard-hearted; I will give out
divers schedules of my beauty: it shall be inventoried,
and every particle and utensil labell'd to my will: — as,
item, two lips, indifferent red; item, two grey eyes, with
lids to them; item, one neck, one chin, and so forth.
Were you sent hither to 'praise me?

VIOLA

I see you what you are, — you are too proud;
But, if you were the devil, you are fair.
My lord and master loves you: O, such love
Could be but recompens'd, though you were crown'd
The nonpareil of beauty!

OLIVIA

How does he love me?

24

VIOLA

With adorations, with fertile tears,
With groans that thunder love, with sighs of fire.

OLIVIA

Your lord does know my mind; I cannot love him:
Yet I suppose him virtuous, know him noble,
Of great estate, of fresh and stainless youth;
In voices well divulg'd, free, learn'd, and valiant;
And, in dimension and the shape of nature,
A gracious person: but yet I cannot love him;
He might have took his answer long ago.

VIOLA

If I did love you in my master's flame,
With such a suffering, such a deadly life,
In your denial I would find no sense;
I would not understand it.

OLIVIA

Why, what would you?

VIOLA

Make me a willow cabin at your gate,
And call upon my soul within the house;
Write loyal cantons of contemned love,
And sing them loud even in the dead of night;
Holla your name to the reverberate hills,
And make the babbling gossip of the air
Cry out, 'Olivia!' O, you should not rest
Between the elements of air and earth,
But you should pity me!

OLIVIA

You might do much. What is your parentage?

VIOLA

Above my fortunes, yet my state is well:
I am a gentleman.

OLIVIA

Get you to your lord;
I cannot love him: let him send no more;
Unless, perchance, you come to me again,

To tell me how he takes it. Fare you well:
I thank you for your pains: spend this for me.

VIOLA

I am no fee'd post, lady; keep your purse:
My master, not myself, lacks recompense.
Love make his heart of flint, that you shall love;
And let your fervour, like my master's, be
Plac'd in contempt! Farewell, fair cruelty.   [*Exit.*

OLIVIA

'What is your parentage?'
'Above my fortunes, yet my state is well:
I am a gentleman.' I'll be sworn thou art;
Thy tongue, thy face, thy limbs, actions, and spirit,
Do give thee fivefold blazon: — not too fast; —
Soft, soft! —
Unless the master were the man. — How now!
Even so quickly may one catch the plague?
Methinks I feel this youth's perfections
With an invisible and subtle stealth
To creep in at mine eyes. Well, let it be. —
What, ho, Malvolio!

Enter MALVOLIO.

MALVOLIO

        Here, madam, at your service.

OLIVIA

Run after that same peevish messenger,
The county's man: he left this ring behind him,
Would I or not: tell him I'll none of it.
Desire him not to flatter with his lord,
Nor hold him up with hopes; I am not for him:
If that the youth will come this way to-morrow,
I'll give him reasons for't. Hie thee, Malvolio.

MALVOLIO

Madam, I will.   [*Exit.*

OLIVIA

I do I know not what; and fear to find
Mine eye too great a flatterer for my mind.

Fate, show thy force: ourselves we do not owe;
What is decreed must be, — and be this so!   [*Exit.*

ACT II

SCENE I

The sea-coast.

Enter ANTONIO *and* SEBASTIAN.

ANTONIO

Will you stay no longer? nor will you not that I go with
you?

SEBASTIAN

By your patience, no. My stars shine darkly over me: the
malignancy of my fate might perhaps distemper yours;
therefore I shall crave of you your leave that I may bear
my evils alone: it were a bad recompense for your love,
to lay any of them on you.

ANTONIO

Let me yet know of you whither you are bound.

SEBASTIAN

No, sooth, sir: my determinate voyage is mere
extravagancy. But I perceive in you so excellent a touch
of modesty, that you will not extort from me what I am
willing to keep in; therefore it charges me in manners
the rather to express myself. You must know of me,
then, Antonio, my name is Sebastian, which I call'd
Roderigo. My father was that Sebastian of Messaline,
whom I know you have heard of. He left behind him
myself and a sister, both born in an hour: if the heavens
had been pleased, would we had so ended! but you, sir,
altered that; for some hour before you took me from the
breach of the sea was my sister drown'd.

ANTONIO

Alas the day!

SEBASTIAN

A lady, sir, though it was said she much resembled me, was yet of many accounted beautiful: but, though I could not, with such estimable wonder, overfar believe that, yet thus far I will boldly publish her, — she bore a mind that envy could not but call fair. She is drown'd already, sir, with salt water, though I seem to drown her remembrance again with more.

ANTONIO

Pardon me, sir, your bad entertainment.

SEBASTIAN

O good Antonio, forgive me your trouble!

ANTONIO

If you will not murder me for my love, let me be your servant.

SEBASTIAN

If you will not undo what you have done, that is, kill him whom you have recover'd, desire it not. Fare ye well at once: my bosom is full of kindness; and I am yet so near the manners of my mother, that, upon the least occasion more, mine eyes will tell tales of me. I am bound to the Count Orsino's court: farewell.   [*Exit.*

ANTONIO

The gentleness of all the gods go with thee!
I have many enemies in Orsino's court,
Else would I very shortly see thee there:
But, come what may, I do adore thee so,
That danger shall seem sport, and I will go.   [*Exit.*

SCENE II

A street.

Enter VIOLA, MALVOLIO *following.*

MALVOLIO

Were not you even now with the Countess Olivia?

VIOLA

Even now, sir; on a moderate pace I have since arrived but hither.

MALVOLIO

She returns this ring to you, sir: you might have saved
me my pains, to have taken it away yourself. She adds,
moreover, that you should put your lord into a desperate
assurance she will none of him: and one thing more, that
you be never so hardy to come again in his affairs, unless
it be to report your lord's taking of this. Receive it so.

VIOLA

She took no ring of me; — I'll none of it.

MALVOLIO

Come, sir, you peevishly threw it to her; and her will is,
it should be so return'd: if it be worth stooping for, there
it lies in your eye; if not, be it his that finds it.   [*Exit.*

VIOLA

I left no ring with her: what means this lady?
Fortune forbid, my outside have not charm'd her!
She made good view of me; indeed, so much,
That, sure, methought, her eyes had lost her tongue,
For she did speak in starts distractedly.
She loves me, sure; the cunning of her passion
Invites me in this churlish messenger.
None of my lord's ring! why, he sent her none.
I am the man: if it be so, as 'tis,

SEBASTIAN I am bound to the Count Orsino's court: farewell.

Poor lady, she were better love a dream.
Disguise, I see, thou art a wickedness,
Wherein the pregnant enemy does much.
How easy is it for the proper-false
In women's waxen hearts to set their forms!
Alas, our frailty is the cause, not we!
For such as we are made of, such we be.
How will this fadge? my master loves her dearly;
And I, poor monster, fond as much on him;
And she, mistaken, seems to dote on me.
What will become of this? As I am man,
My state is desperate for my master's love;
As I am woman, — now, alas the day! —
What thriftless sighs shall poor Olivia breathe!
O Time, thou must untangle this, not I;
It is too hard a knot for me t'untie!   [*Exit.*

SCENE III

Olivia's house.

Enter SIR TOBY *and* SIR ANDREW.

SIR TOBY

Approach, Sir Andrew: not to be a-bed after midnight is
to be up betimes; and *diluculo surgere*, thou know'st, —

SIR ANDREW

Nay, by my troth, I know not: but I know, to be up late
is to be up late.

SIR TOBY

A false conclusion: I hate it as an unfill'd can. To be up
after midnight, and to go to bed then, is early: so that to
go to bed after midnight is to go to bed betimes. Does
not our life consist of the four elements?

SIR ANDREW

Faith, so they say; but, I think, it rather consists of
eating and drinking.

SIR TOBY

Th'art a scholar: let us therefore eat and drink. —
Marian, I say! a stoup of wine!

SIR ANDREW

Here comes the fool, i'faith.

Enter CLOWN.

CLOWN

How now, my hearts! did you never see the picture of
We Three?

SIR TOBY

Welcome, ass. Now let's have a catch.

SIR ANDREW

By my troth, the fool has an excellent breast. I had
rather than forty shillings I had such a leg, and so sweet
a breath to sing, as the fool has. In sooth, thou wast in
very gracious fooling last night, when thou spokest of
Pigrogromitus, of the Vapians passing the equinoctial of
Queubus: 'twas very good, i'faith. I sent thee sixpence
for thy leman: hadst it?

CLOWN

I did impeticos thy gratillity; for Malvolio's nose is no
whipstock; my lady has a white hand, and the
Myrmidons are no bottle-ale houses.

SIR ANDREW

Excellent! why, this is the best fooling, when all is done.
Now, a song.

SIR TOBY

Come on; there is sixpence for you: let's have a song.

SIR ANDREW

There's a testril of me too; if one knight give a —

CLOWN

Would you have a love-song, or a song of good life?

SIR TOBY

A love-song, a love-song.

SIR ANDREW

Ay, ay: I care not for good life.

CLOWN [*sings*].

    O mistress mine, where are you roaming?
    O, stay and hear; your true-love's coming,
        That can sing both high and low:
    Trip no further, pretty sweeting;
    Journeys end in lovers' meeting,
        Every wise man's son doth know.

SIR ANDREW

Excellent good, i'faith.

SIR TOBY

Good, good.

CLOWN

    What is love? 'tis not hereafter;
    Present mirth hath present laughter;
        What's to come is still unsure:
    In delay there lies no plenty;
    Then come kiss me, sweet-and-twenty,
        Youth's a stuff will not endure.

SIR ANDREW

A mellifluous voice, as I am true knight.

SIR TOBY

A contagious breath.

SIR ANDREW

Very sweet and contagious, i'faith.

SIR TOBY

To hear by the nose, it is dulcet in contagion. But shall
we make the welkin dance indeed? shall we rouse the
night-owl in a catch that will draw three souls out of one
weaver? shall we do that?

SIR ANDREW

An you love me, let's do't: I am dog at a catch.

CLOWN

By'r lady, sir, and some dogs will catch well.

SIR ANDREW

Most certain. Let our catch be, 'Thou knave.'

CLOWN

'Hold thy peace, thou knave,' knight? I shall be
constrain'd in't to call thee knave, knight.

SIR ANDREW

'Tis not the first time I have constrain'd one to call me
knave. Begin, fool: it begins, 'Hold thy peace.'

CLOWN

I shall never begin, if I hold my peace.

SIR ANDREW

Good, i'faith. Come, begin.   [*Catch sung.*

Enter MARIA.

MARIA

What a caterwauling do you keep here! If my lady have
not call'd up her steward Malvolio, and bid him turn
you out of doors, never trust me.

SIR TOBY

My lady's a Cataian, we are politicians, Malvolio's a
Peg-a-Ramsey, and 'Three merry men be we.' Am not I
consanguineous? am I not of her blood? Tilly-vally, lady!
[*Sings*] 'There dwelt a man in Babylon, lady, lady!'

CLOWN

Beshrew me, the knight's in admirable fooling.

SIR ANDREW

Ay, he does well enough if he be disposed, and so do I
too: he does it with a better grace, but I do it more
natural.

SIR TOBY

'O, the twelfth day of December, —'

MARIA

For the love o' God, peace!

Enter MALVOLIO.

MALVOLIO

My masters, are you mad? or what are you? Have you
no wit, manners, nor honesty, but to gabble like tinkers
at this time of night? Do ye make an ale-house of my
lady's house, that ye squeak out your cosiers' catches

33

without any mitigation or remorse of voice? Is there no respect of place, persons, nor time, in you?

SIR TOBY

We did keep time, sir, in our catches. Sneck-up!

MALVOLIO

Sir Toby, I must be round with you. My lady bade me tell you, that, though she harbours you as her kinsman, she's nothing allied to your disorders. If you can separate yourself and your misdemeanours, you are welcome to the house; if not, an it would please you to take leave of her, she is very willing to bid you farewell.

MALVOLIO Is there no respect of place, persons, nor time, in you?

SIR TOBY

'Farewell, dear heart, since I must needs be gone.'

MARIA

Nay, good Sir Toby.

CLOWN

'His eyes do show his days are almost done.'

MALVOLIO

Is't even so?

SIR TOBY

'But I will never die.'

CLOWN

Sir Toby, there you lie.

MALVOLIO

This is much credit to you.

SIR TOBY

'Shall I bid him go?'

CLOWN

'What an if you do?'

SIR TOBY

'Shall I bid him go, and spare not?'

CLOWN

'O, no, no, no, no, you dare not.'

SIR TOBY

Out o' time, sir? ye lie. — Art any more than a steward?
Dost thou think, because thou art virtuous, there shall
be no more cakes and ale?

CLOWN

Yes, by Saint Anne; and ginger shall be hot i'th'mouth
too.

SIR TOBY

Th'art i'th'right. — Go, sir, rub your chain with
crumbs. — A stoup of wine, Maria!

MALVOLIO

Mistress Mary, if you prized my lady's favour at any
thing more than contempt, you would not give means
for this uncivil rule: she shall know of it, by this hand.

35

[*Exit.*

MARIA

Go shake your ears.

SIR ANDREW

'Twere as good a deed as to drink when a man's a-hungry, to challenge him the field, and then to break promise with him, and make a fool of him.

SIR TOBY

Do't, knight: I'll write thee a challenge; or I'll deliver thy indignation to him by word of mouth.

MARIA

Sweet Sir Toby, be patient for to-night; since the youth of the count's was to-day with my lady, she is much out of quiet. For Monsieur Malvolio, let me alone with him: if I do not gull him into a nayword, and make him a common recreation, do not think I have wit enough to lie straight in my bed: I know I can do it.

SIR TOBY

Possess us, possess us; tell us something of him.

MARIA

Marry, sir, sometimes he is a kind of puritan.

SIR ANDREW

O, if I thought that I'ld beat him like a dog!

SIR TOBY

What, for being a puritan? thy exquisite reason, dear knight?

SIR ANDREW

I have no exquisite reason for't, but I have reason good enough.

MARIA

The devil a puritan that he is, or any thing constantly, but a time-pleaser; an affection'd ass, that cons state without book, and utters it by great swarths: the best persuaded of himself, so cramm'd, as he thinks, with excellencies, that it is his grounds of faith that all that

look on him love him; and on that vice in him will my
revenge find notable cause to work.

SIR TOBY

What wilt thou do?

MARIA

I will drop in his way some obscure epistles of love;
wherein, by the colour of his beard, the shape of his leg,
the manner of his gait, the expressure of his eye,
forehead, and complexion, he shall find himself most
feelingly personated: I can write very like my lady, your
niece; on a forgotten matter we can hardly make
distinction of our hands.

SIR TOBY

Excellent! I smell a device.

SIR ANDREW

I have't in my nose too.

SIR TOBY

He shall think, by the letters that thou wilt drop, that they
come from my niece, and that she's in love with him.

MARIA

My purpose is, indeed, a horse of that colour.

SIR TOBY

And your horse now would make him an ass.

MARIA

Ass, I doubt not.

SIR ANDREW

O, 'twill be admirable!

MARIA

Sport royal, I warrant you: I know my physic will work
with him. I will plant you two, and let the fool make a
third, where he shall find the letter: observe his
construction of it. For this night, to bed, and dream on
the event. Farewell.

SIR TOBY

Good night, Penthesilea.   [*Exit* MARIA.

SIR ANDREW

Before me, she's a good wench.

SIR TOBY

She's a beagle, true-bred, and one that adores me: what o' that?

SIR ANDREW

I was adored once too.

SIR TOBY

Let's to bed, knight. — Thou hadst need send for more money.

SIR ANDREW

If I cannot recover your niece, I am a foul way out.

SIR TOBY

Send for money, knight: if thou hast her not i'th'end, call me cut.

SIR ANDREW

If I do not, never trust me, take it how you will.

SIR TOBY

Come, come; I'll go burn some sack; 'tis too late to go to bed now: come, knight; come, knight.　　　　[*Exeunt.*

SCENE IV

The DUKE'S *palace.*

Enter DUKE, VIOLA, CURIO, *and others.*

DUKE

Give me some music: — now, good morrow, friends: —
Now, good Cesario, but that piece of song,
That old and antique song we heard last night:
Methought it did relieve my passion much,
More than light airs and recollected terms
Of these most brisk and giddy-paced times —
Come, but one verse.

CURIO

He is not here, so please your lordship, that should sing it.

DUKE

Who was it?

CURIO

Feste, the jester, my lord; a fool that the Lady Olivia's
father took much delight in: he is about the house.

DUKE

Seek him out: and play the tune the while.

[*Exit* CURIO. *Music plays.*

Come hither, boy: if ever thou shalt love,
In the sweet pangs of it remember me;
For such as I am all true lovers are,
Unstaid and skittish in all motions else,
Save in the constant image of the creature
That is beloved. — How dost thou like this tune?

VIOLA

It gives a very echo to the seat
Where Love is thron'd.

DUKE

Thou dost speak masterly:
My life upon't, young though thou art, thine eye
Hath stay'd upon some favour that it loves; —
Hath it not, boy?

VIOLA

A little, by your favour.

DUKE

What kind of woman is't?

VIOLA

Of your complexion.

DUKE

She is not worth thee, then. What years, i'faith?

VIOLA

About your years, my lord.

DUKE

Too old, by heaven: let still the woman take
An elder than herself; so wears she to him,
So sways she level in her husband's heart:
For, boy, however we do praise ourselves,

Our fancies are more giddy and unfirm,
More longing, wavering, sooner lost and worn,
Than women's are.

VIOLA

               I think it well, my lord.

DUKE

Then let thy love be younger than thyself,
Or thy affection cannot hold the bent;
For women are as roses, whose fair flower
Being once display'd, doth fall that very hour.

VIOLA

And so they are: alas, that they are so, —
To die, even when they to perfection grow!

        Enter CURIO *and* CLOWN.

DUKE

O, fellow, come, the song we had last night. —
Mark it, Cesario; it is old and plain:
The spinsters and the knitters in the sun,
And the free maids that weave their thread with bones,
Do use to chant it: it is silly sooth,
And dallies with the innocence of love,
Like the old age.

CLOWN

Are you ready, sir?

DUKE

Ay; prithee, sing.   [*Music.*

CLOWN

    Come away, come away, death,
        And in sad cypress let me be laid;
    Fly away, fly away, breath;
        I am slain by a fair cruel maid.
    My shroud of white, stuck all with yew,
        O, prepare it!
    My part of death, no one so true
        Did share it.
    Not a flower, not a flower sweet,

> On my black coffin let there be strown;
> Not a friend, not a friend greet
>> My poor corpse, where my bones shall be
>> thrown:
> A thousand thousand sighs to save,
>> Lay me, O, where
> Sad true lover never find my grave,
>> To weep there!

DUKE

There's for thy pains.

CLOWN

No pains, sir; I take pleasure in singing, sir.

DUKE

I'll pay thy pleasure, then.

CLOWN

Truly, sir, and pleasure will be paid, one time or
another.

DUKE

Give me now leave to leave thee.

CLOWN

Now, the melancholy god protect thee; and the tailor
make thy doublet of changeable taffeta, for thy mind is a
very opal! I would have men of such constancy put to sea,
that their business might be every thing, and their intent
every where; for that's it that always makes a good voyage
of nothing. Farewell.   [*Exit.*

DUKE

Let all the rest give place.

>> [*Exeunt* CURIO *and* ATTENDANTS.
>> Once more, Cesario,
> Get thee to yond same sovereign cruelty:
> Tell her, my love, more noble than the world,
> Prizes not quantity of dirty lands;
> The parts that Fortune hath bestow'd upon her,
> Tell her, I hold as giddily as Fortune;
> But 'tis that miracle and queen of gems,
> That nature pranks her in, attracts my soul.

VIOLA

But if she cannot love you, sir?

DUKE

I cannot be so answer'd.

VIOLA

              Sooth, but you must.
Say that some lady — as, perhaps, there is —
Hath for your love as great a pang of heart
As you have for Olivia: you cannot love her;
You tell her so; must she not, then, be answer'd?

DUKE

There is no woman's sides
Can bide the beating of so strong a passion
As love doth give my heart; no woman's heart
So big, to hold so much; they lack retention.
Alas, their love may be call'd appetite, —
No motion of the liver, but the palate, —
That suffer surfeit, cloyment, and revolt;
But mine is all as hungry as the sea,
And can digest as much: make no compare
Between that love a woman can bear me
And that I owe Olivia.

VIOLA

              Ay, but I know, —

DUKE

What dost thou know?

VIOLA

Too well what love women to men may owe:
In faith, they are as true of heart as we.
My father had a daughter lov'd a man,
As it might be, perhaps, were I a woman,
I should your lordship.

DUKE

              And what's her history?

VIOLA

A blank, my lord. She never told her love,
But let concealment, like a worm i'th'bud,

42

Feed on her damask cheek: she pin'd in thought;
And, with a green and yellow melancholy,
She sat like Patience on a monument,
Smiling at grief. Was not this love indeed?
We men may say more, swear more: but, indeed,
Our shows are more than will; for still we prove
Much in our vows, but little in our love.

DUKE

But died thy sister of her love, my boy?

VIOLA

I am all the daughters of my father's house,
And all the brothers too; — and yet I know not. —
Sir, shall I to this lady?

DUKE

           Ay, that's the theme.
To her in haste; give her this jewel; say,
My love can give no place, bide no denay.   [*Exeunt.*

SCENE V

OLIVIA'S *garden.*

Enter SIR TOBY, SIR ANDREW, *and* FABIAN.

SIR TOBY

Come thy ways, Signior Fabian.

FABIAN

Nay, I'll come: if I lose a scruple of this sport, let me be
boil'd to death with melancholy.

SIR TOBY

Wouldst thou not be glad to have the niggardly rascally
sheep-biter come by some notable shame?

FABIAN

I would exult, man: you know he brought me out o'
favour with my lady about a bear-baiting here.

SIR TOBY

To anger him, we'll have the bear again; and we will fool
him black and blue: — shall we not, Sir Andrew?

SIR ANDREW

An we do not, it is pity of our lives.

SIR TOBY

Here comes the little villain.

Enter MARIA.

How now, my metal of India!

MARIA

Get ye all three into the box-tree: Malvolio's coming
down this walk: he has been yonder i' the sun practising
behaviour to his own shadow this half-hour: observe him,
for the love of mockery; for I know this letter will make a
contemplative idiot of him. Close, in the name of jesting!
Lie thou there [*throws down a letter*]; for here comes the
trout that must be caught with tickling. [*Exit.*

MARIA Get ye all three into the box-tree: Malvolio's coming down this walk

Enter MALVOLIO.

MALVOLIO

'Tis but fortune; all is fortune. Maria once told me she did affect me: and I have heard herself come thus near, that, should she fancy, it should be one of my complexion. Besides, she uses me with a more exalted respect than any one else that follows her. What should I think on't?

SIR TOBY

Here's an overweening rogue!

FABIAN

O, peace! Contemplation makes a rare turkey-cock of him: how he jets under his advanced plumes!

SIR ANDREW

'Slight, I could so beat the rogue!

SIR TOBY

Peace, I say.

MALVOLIO

To be Count Malvolio, —

SIR TOBY

Ah, rogue!

SIR ANDREW

Pistol him, pistol him.

SIR TOBY

Peace, peace!

MALVOLIO

There is example for't; the lady of the Strachy married the yeoman of the wardrobe.

SIR ANDREW

Fie on him, Jezebel!

FABIAN

O, peace! now he's deeply in: look how imagination blows him.

MALVOLIO

Having been three months married to her, sitting in my state, —

45

SIR TOBY

O, for a stone-bow, to hit him in the eye!

MALVOLIO

Calling my officers about me, in my branch'd velvet gown; having come from a day-bed, where I have left Olivia sleeping, —

SIR TOBY

Fire and brimstone!

FABIAN

O, peace, peace!

MALVOLIO

And then to have the humour of state; and after a demure travel of regard, — telling them I know my place, as I would they should do theirs, — to ask for my kinsman Toby, —

SIR TOBY

Bolts and shackles!

FABIAN

O, peace, peace, peace! now, now.

MALVOLIO

Seven of my people, with an obedient start, make out for him: I frown the while; and perchance wind up my watch, or play with some rich jewel. Toby approaches; court'sies there to me, —

SIR TOBY

Shall this fellow live?

FABIAN

Though our silence be drawn from us with cars, yet peace.

MALVOLIO

I extend my hand to him thus, quenching my familiar smile with an austere regard of control,—

SIR TOBY

And does not Toby take you a blow o' the lips then?

MALVOLIO

Saying, 'Cousin Toby, my fortunes having cast me on
your niece, give me this prerogative of speech,' —

SIR TOBY

What, what?

MALVOLIO

'You must amend your drunkenness.'

SIR TOBY

Out, scab!

FABIAN

Nay, patience, or we break the sinews of our plot.

MALVOLIO

'Besides, you waste the treasure of your time with a
foolish knight,' —

SIR ANDREW

That's me, I warrant you.

MALVOLIO

'One Sir Andrew,' —

SIR ANDREW

I knew 'twas I; for many do call me fool.

MALVOLIO

What employment have we here?   [*Taking up the letter.*

FABIAN

Now is the woodcock near the gin.

SIR TOBY

O peace! and the spirit of humours intimate reading
aloud to him!

MALVOLIO

By my life, this is my lady's hand: these be her very C's,
her U's, and her T's; and thus makes she her great P's.
It is, in contempt of question, her hand.

SIR ANDREW

Her C's, her U's, and her T's: why that?

MALVOLIO [*reads*].

To the unknown beloved, this, and my good wishes: her
very phrases! — By your leave, wax. — Soft! — and the

47

impressure her Lucrece, with which she uses to seal: 'tis
my lady. To whom should this be?

FABIAN

This wins him, liver and all.

MALVOLIO [*reads*].

    Jove knows I love:
        But who?
    Lips, do not move;
No man must know.

'No man must know.' — What follows? the numbers
alter'd! — 'No man must know': — if this should be
thee, Malvolio?

SIR TOBY

Marry, hang thee, brock!

MALVOLIO [*reads*].

    I may command where I adore;
        But silence, like a Lucrece knife,
    With bloodless stroke my heart doth gore:
        M, O, A, I, doth sway my life.

FABIAN

A fustian riddle!

SIR TOBY

Excellent wench, say I.

MALVOLIO

'M, O, A, I, doth sway my life.' — Nay, but first, let me
see, — let me see, — let me see.

FABIAN

What dish o' poison has she dress'd him!

SIR TOBY

And with what wing the staniel checks at it!

MALVOLIO

'I may command where I adore.' Why, she may
command me: I serve her; she is my lady. Why, this is
evident to any formal capacity; there is no obstruction in
this: — and the end, — what should that alphabetical
position portend? if I could make that resemble
something in me, — Softly! — M, O, A, I, —

SIR TOBY

O, ay, make up that: — he is now at a cold scent.

FABIAN

Sowter will cry upon't, for all this, though it be as rank
as a fox.

MALVOLIO

M, — Malvolio; — M, — why, that begins my name.

FABIAN

Did not I say he would work it out? the cur is excellent
at faults.

MALVOLIO

M, — but then there is no consonancy in the sequel;
that suffers under probation: A should follow, but O
does.

FABIAN

And O shall end, I hope.

SIR TOBY

Ay, or I'll cudgel him, and make him cry O!

MALVOLIO

And then I comes behind.

FABIAN

Ay, an you had any eye behind you, you might see more
detraction at your heels than fortunes before you.

MALVOLIO

M, O, A, I; — this simulation is not as the former: —
and yet, to crush this a little, it would bow to me, for
every one of these letters are in my name. Soft! here
follows prose. — [*reads*] 'If this fall into thy hand,
revolve. In my stars I am above thee; but be not afraid of
greatness: some are born great, some achieve greatness,
and some have greatness thrust upon 'em. Thy Fates
open their hands; let thy blood and spirit embrace them:
and, to inure thyself to what thou art like to be, cast thy
humble slough, and appear fresh.
Be opposite with a kinsman, surly with servants;
let thy tongue tang arguments of state; put thyself
into the trick of singularity: she thus advises thee

49

that sighs for thee. Remember who commended thy
yellow stockings, and wish'd to see thee ever cross-
garter'd: I say, remember. Go to, thou art made, if thou
desirest to be so; if not, let me see thee a steward still, the
fellow of servants, and not worthy to touch Fortune's
fingers. Farewell. She that would alter services with thee,

THE FORTUNATE-UNHAPPY.'

Daylight and champain discovers not more: this is open. I
will be proud, I will read politic authors, I will baffle Sir
Toby, I will wash off gross acquaintance, I will be point-
devise the very man. I do not now fool myself, to let imagination jade me; for every reason excites to this, that my lady
loves me. She did commend my yellow stockings of late,
she did praise my leg being cross-garter'd; and in this she
manifests herself to my love, and, with a kind of injunction,
drives me to these habits of her liking. I thank my stars, I
am happy. I will be strange, stout, in yellow stockings, and
cross-garter'd, even with the swiftness of putting on. Jove
and my stars be praised! — Here is yet a postscript. [*reads*]
'Thou canst not choose but know who I am. If thou
entertain'st my love, let it appear in thy smiling: thy smiles
become thee well; therefore in my presence still smile, dear
my sweet, I prithee.' Jove, I thank thee: — I will smile; I will
do every thing that thou wilt have me.   [*Exit.*

FABIAN
I will not give my part of this sport for a pension of
thousands to be paid from the Sophy.

SIR TOBY
I could marry this wench for this device, —

SIR ANDREW
So could I too.

SIR TOBY
And ask no other dowry with her but such another jest.

SIR ANDREW
Nor I neither.

FABIAN
Here comes my noble gull-catcher.

MALVOLIO I will smile; I will do every thing that thou wilt have me.

Enter MARIA.

SIR TOBY

Wilt thou set thy foot o'my neck?

SIR ANDREW

Or o' mine either?

SIR TOBY

Shall I play my freedom at tray-trip, and become thy bond-slave?

SIR ANDREW

I'faith, or I either?

SIR TOBY

Why, thou hast put him in such a dream, that, when the image of it leaves him, he must run mad.

MARIA

Nay, but say true; does it work upon him?

SIR TOBY

Like aqua-vitæ with a midwife.

MARIA

If you will then see the fruits of the sport, mark his first approach before my lady: he will come to her in yellow stockings, and 'tis a colour she abhors, and cross-garter'd, a fashion she detests; and he will smile upon her, which will now be so unsuitable to her disposition, being addicted to a melancholy as she is, that it cannot but turn him into a notable contempt. If you will see it, follow me.

SIR TOBY

To the gates of Tartar, thou most excellent devil of wit!

SIR ANDREW

I'll make one too.   [*Exeunt.*

ACT III

SCENE I

OLIVIA'S *garden.*

Enter VIOLA, *and* CLOWN *with a tabor.*

VIOLA

Save thee, friend, and thy music! dost thou live by thy tabor?

CLOWN

No, sir, I live by the church.

VIOLA

Art thou a churchman?

CLOWN

No such matter, sir: I do live by the church; for I do
live at my house, and my house doth stand by the
church.

VIOLA

So thou mayst say, the king lies by a beggar, if a beggar
dwell near him; or, the church stands by thy tabor, if thy
tabor stand by the church.

CLOWN

You have said, sir. — To see this age! A sentence is but
a cheveril glove to a good wit: how quickly the wrong
side may be turn'd outward!

VIOLA

Nay, that's certain; they that dally nicely with words
may quickly make them wanton.

CLOWN

I would, therefore, my sister had had no name, sir.

VIOLA

Why, man?

CLOWN

Why, sir, her name's a word; and to dally with that word
might make my sister wanton. But, indeed, words are
very rascals, since bonds disgraced them.

VIOLA

Thy reason, man?

CLOWN

Troth, sir, I can yield you none without words; and
words are grown so false, I am loth to prove reason with
them.

VIOLA

I warrant thou art a merry fellow, and carest for nothing.

CLOWN

Not so, sir; I do care for something; but in my
conscience, sir, I do not care for you: if that be to care
for nothing, sir, I would it would make you invisible.

VIOLA

Art not thou the Lady Olivia's fool?

CLOWN

No, indeed, sir; the Lady Olivia has no folly: she will
keep no fool, sir, till she be married; and fools are as like
husbands as pilchers are to herrings, — the husband's
the bigger: I am, indeed, not her fool, but her corrupter
of words.

VIOLA

I saw thee late at the Count Orsino's.

CLOWN

Foolery, sir, does walk about the orb like the sun, it
shines every where. I would be sorry, sir, but the fool
should be as oft with your master as with my mistress: I
think I saw your wisdom there.

VIOLA

Nay, an thou pass upon me, I'll no more with thee.
Hold, there's expenses for thee.

CLOWN

Now Jove, in his next commodity of hair, send thee a
beard!

VIOLA

By my troth, I'll tell thee, I am almost sick for one:
though I would not have it grow on my chin. Is thy lady
within?

CLOWN

Would not a pair of these have bred, sir?

VIOLA

Yes, being kept together and put to use.

CLOWN

I would play Lord Pandarus of Phrygia, sir, to bring a
Cressida to this Troilus.

VIOLA

I understand you, sir; 'tis well begg'd.

CLOWN

The matter, I hope, is not great, sir, begging but a beggar:
Cressida was a beggar. My lady is within, sir. I will conster
to them whence you come; who you are, and what you
would, are out of my welkin, — I might say element, but
the word is over-worn. [*Exit.*

VIOLA

This fellow is wise enough to play the fool;
And to do that well craves a kind of wit:
He must observe their mood on whom he jests,
The quality of persons, and the time;
Not, like the haggard, check at every feather
That comes before his eye. This is a practice
As full of labour as a wise man's art:
For folly, that he wisely shows, is fit;
But wise men, folly-fall'n, quite taint their wit.

Enter SIR TOBY *and* SIR ANDREW.

SIR TOBY

Save you, gentleman!

VIOLA

And you, sir.

SIR ANDREW

Dieu vous garde, monsieur.

VIOLA

Et vous aussi; votre serviteur.

SIR ANDREW

I hope, sir, you are; and I am yours.

SIR TOBY

Will you encounter the house? my niece is desirous you
should enter, if your trade be to her.

VIOLA

I am bound to your niece, sir; I mean, she is the list of
my voyage.

55

SIR TOBY

Taste your legs, sir; put them to motion.

VIOLA

My legs do better understand me, sir, than I understand
what you mean by bidding me taste my legs.

SIR TOBY

I mean, to go, sir, to enter.

VIOLA

I will answer you with gait and entrance: — but we are
prevented.

           Enter OLIVIA *and* MARIA.

Most excellent accomplish'd lady, the heavens rain
odours on you!

SIR ANDREW [*aside*].

That youth's a rare courtier: 'Rain odours': — well.

VIOLA

My matter hath no voice, lady, but to your own most
pregnant and vouchsafed ear.

SIR ANDREW [*aside*].

'Odours,' 'pregnant,' and 'vouchsafed': — I'll get 'em all
three all ready.

OLIVIA

Let the garden-door be shut, and leave me to my
hearing. [*Exeunt* SIR TOBY, SIR ANDREW, *and*
MARIA.] Give me your hand, sir.

VIOLA

My duty, madam, and most humble service.

OLIVIA

What is your name?

VIOLA

Cesario is your servant's name, fair princess.

OLIVIA

My servant, sir! 'Twas never merry world
Since lowly feigning was call'd compliment:
Y'are servant to the Count Orsino, youth.

VIOLA

And he is yours, and his must needs be yours:
Your servant's servant is your servant, madam.

OLIVIA

For him, I think not on him: for his thoughts,
Would they were blanks, rather than fill'd with me!

VIOLA

Madam, I come to whet your gentle thoughts
On his behalf: —

OLIVIA

        O, by your leave, I pray you, —
I bade you never speak again of him:
But, would you undertake another suit,
I had rather hear you to solicit that
Than music from the spheres.

VIOLA

        Dear lady, —

OLIVIA

Give me leave, beseech you. I did send,
After the last enchantment you did here,
A ring in chase of you: so did I abuse
Myself, my servant, and, I fear me, you:
Under your hard construction must I sit,
To force that on you, in a shameful cunning,
Which you knew none of yours: what might you think?
Have you not set mine honour at the stake,
And baited it with all th'unmuzzled thoughts
That tyrannous heart can think? To one of your
    receiving
Enough is shown: a cypress, not a bosom,
Hides my poor heart. So, let me hear you speak.

VIOLA

I pity you.

OLIVIA

        That's a degree to love.

VIOLA

No, not a grise; for 'tis a vulgar proof,

57

That very oft we pity enemies.

OLIVIA

Why, then, methinks 'tis time to smile again.
O world, how apt the poor are to be proud!
If one should be a prey, how much the better
To fall before the lion than the wolf!   *[Clock strikes.*
The clock upbraids me with the waste of time. —
Be not afraid, good youth, I will not have you:
And yet, when wit and youth is come to harvest,
Your wife is like to reap a proper man:
There lies your way, due west.

VIOLA

                     Then westward-ho! —
Grace and good disposition attend your ladyship!
You'll nothing, madam, to my lord by me?

OLIVIA

Stay:
I prithee, tell me what thou think'st of me.

VIOLA

That you do think you are not what you are.

OLIVIA

If I think so, I think the same of you.

VIOLA

Then think you right: I am not what I am.

OLIVIA

I would you were as I would have you be!

VIOLA

Would it be better, madam, than I am,
I wish it might; for now I am your fool.

OLIVIA

O, what a deal of scorn looks beautiful
In the contempt and anger of his lip!
A murderous guilt shows not itself more soon
Than love that would seem hid: love's night is noon.
Cesario, by the roses of the spring,
By maidhood, honour, truth, and every thing,

58

I love thee so, that, maugre all thy pride,
Nor wit nor reason can my passion hide.
Do not extort thy reasons from this clause,
For that I woo, thou therefore hast no cause;
But, rather, reason thus with reason fetter, —
Love sought is good, but given unsought is better.

VIOLA

By innocence I swear, and by my youth,
I have one heart, one bosom, and one truth, —
And that no woman has; nor never none
Shall mistress be of it, save I alone.
And so adieu, good madam: never more
Will I my master's tears to you deplore.

OLIVIA

Yet come again; for thou perhaps mayst move
That heart, which now abhors, to like his love.

[*Exeunt.*

SCENE II

OLIVIA'S *house.*

Enter SIR TOBY, SIR ANDREW, *and* FABIAN.

SIR ANDREW

No, faith, I'll not stay a jot longer.

SIR TOBY

Thy reason, dear venom; give thy reason.

FABIAN

You must needs yield your reason, Sir Andrew.

SIR ANDREW

Marry, I saw your niece do more favours to the count's
serving-man than ever she bestow'd upon me; I saw't
i'th'orchard.

SIR TOBY

Did she see thee the while, old boy? tell me that.

SIR ANDREW

As plain as I see you now.

59

FABIAN

This was a great argument of love in her toward you.

SIR ANDREW

'Slight, will you make an ass o'me?

FABIAN

I will prove it legitimate, sir, upon the oaths of judgement and reason.

SIR TOBY

And they have been grand-jurymen since before Noah was a sailor.

FABIAN

She did show favour to the youth in your sight only to exasperate you, to awake your dormouse valour, to put fire in your heart, and brimstone in your liver. You should then have accosted her; and with some excellent jests, fire-new from the mint, you should have bang'd the youth into dumbness. This was look'd for at your hand, and this was balk'd: the double gilt of this opportunity you let time wash off, and you are now sail'd into the north of my lady's opinion; where you will hang like an icicle on a Dutchman's beard, unless you do redeem it by some laudable attempt either of valour or policy.

SIR ANDREW

An't be any way, it must be with valour; for policy I hate: I had as lief be a Brownist as a politician.

SIR TOBY

Why, then, build me thy fortunes upon the basis of valour. Challenge me the count's youth to fight with him; hurt him in eleven places: my niece shall take note of it; and assure thyself, there is no love-broker in the world can more prevail in man's commendation with woman than report of valour.

FABIAN

There is no way but this, Sir Andrew.

SIR ANDREW

Will either of you bear me a challenge to him?

SIR TOBY

Go, write it in a martial hand; be curst and brief; it is no matter how witty, so it be eloquent and full of invention: taunt him with the licence of ink: if thou 'thou'st'him some thrice, it shall not be amiss; and as many lies as will lie in thy sheet of paper, although the sheet were big enough for the bed of Ware in England, set 'em down: go, about it. Let there be gall enough in thy ink, though thou write with a goose-pen, no matter: about it.

SIR ANDREW

Where shall I find you?

SIR TOBY

We'll call thee at the *cubiculo*: go. [*Exit* SIR ANDREW.

FABIAN

This is a dear manakin to you, Sir Toby.

SIR TOBY

I have been dear to him, lad, — some two thousand strong, or so.

FABIAN

We shall have a rare letter from him: but you'll not deliver't?

SIR TOBY

Never trust me, then; and by all means stir on the youth to an answer. I think oxen and wainropes cannot hale them together. For Andrew, if he were open'd, and you find so much blood in his liver as will clog the foot of a flea, I'll eat the rest of th'anatomy.

FABIAN

And his opposite, the youth, bears in his visage no great presage of cruelty.

SIR TOBY

Look, where the youngest wren of nine comes.

Enter MARIA.

MARIA

I you desire the spleen, and will laugh yourselves into stitches, follow me. Yond gull Malvolio is turn'd heathen, a very renegado; for there is no Christian, that means to be saved by believing rightly, can ever believe such impossible passages of grossness. He's in yellow stockings.

SIR TOBY

And cross-garter'd?

MARIA

Most villainously; like a pedant that keeps a school i'th'church. — I have dogg'd him, like his murderer. He does obey every point of the letter that I dropp'd to betray him: he does smile his face into more lines than is in the new map, with the augmentation of the Indies: you have not seen such a thing as 'tis; I can hardly forbear hurling things at him. I know my lady will strike him: if she do, he'll smile, and take't for a great favour.

SIR TOBY

Come, bring us, bring us where he is.   [*Exeunt.*

SCENE III

A street.

Enter SEBASTIAN *and* ANTONIO.

SEBASTIAN

I would not, by my will, have troubled you;
But, since you make your pleasure of your pains,
I will no further chide you.

ANTONIO

I could not stay behind you: my desire,
More sharp than filed steel, did spur me forth;
And not all love to see you, — though so much
As might have drawn me to a longer voyage, —
But jealousy what might befall your travel,
Being skilless in these parts; which to a stranger,
Unguided and unfriended, often prove
Rough and unhospitable: my willing love,
The rather by these arguments of fear,
Set forth in your pursuit.

SEBASTIAN

                    My kind Antonio,
I can no other answer make, but thanks,
And thanks, and ever; oft good turns
Are shuffled off with such uncurrent pay:
But, were my worth, as is my conscience, firm,
You should find better dealing. What's to do?
Shall we go see the reliques of this town?

ANTONIO

To-morrow, sir; best first go see your lodging.

SEBASTIAN

I am not weary, and 'tis long to night:
I pray you, let us satisfy our eyes
With the memorials and the things of fame
That do renown this city.

ANTONIO

                       Would you'ld pardon me;
I do not without danger walk these streets:
Once, in a sea-fight, 'gainst the count his galleys
I did some service; of such note, indeed,
That, were I ta'en here, it would scarce be answer'd.

SEBASTIAN

Belike you slew great number of his people?

ANTONIO

Th'offence is not of such a bloody nature;
Albeit the quality of the time and quarrel
Might well have given us bloody argument.
It might have since been answer'd in repaying
What we took from them; which, for traffic's sake,
Most of our city did: only myself stood out;
For which, if I be lapsed in this place,
I shall pay dear.

SEBASTIAN

                Do not, then, walk too open.

ANTONIO

It doth not fit me. Hold, sir, here's my purse.
In the south suburbs, at the Elephant,

Is best to lodge: I will bespeak our diet,
Whiles you beguile the time and feed your knowledge
With viewing of the town: there shall you have me.

SEBASTIAN

Why I your purse?

ANTONIO

Haply your eye shall light upon some toy
You have desire to purchase; and your store,
I think, is not for idle markets, sir.

SEBASTIAN

I'll be your purse-bearer, and leave you for
An hour.

ANTONIO

       To th'Elephant.

SEBASTIAN

                I do remember.   [*Exeunt.*

SCENE IV

OLIVIA'S *garden.*

Enter OLIVIA *and* MARIA.

OLIVIA

I have sent after him: he says he'll come; —
How shall I feast him? what bestow of him?
For youth is bought more oft than begg'd or borrow'd.
I speak too loud. —
Where is Malvolio? — he is sad and civil,
And suits well for a servant with my fortunes: —
Where is Malvolio?

MARIA

He's coming, madam; but in very strange manner. He
is, sure, possess'd, madam.

OLIVIA

Why, what's the matter? does he rave?

MARIA

No, madam, he does nothing but smile: your ladyship
were best to have some guard about you, if he come; for,
sure, the man is tainted in's wits.

OLIVIA

Go call him hither. [*Exit* MARIA.] I am as mad as he,
If sad and merry madness equal be.

       Enter MARIA, *with* MALVOLIO.

How now, Malvolio!

MALVOLIO

Sweet lady, ho, ho.   [*Smiles fantastically.*

OLIVIA

Smilest thou?
I sent for thee upon a sad occasion.

MALVOLIO

Sad, lady! I could be sad: this does make some
obstruction in the blood, this cross-gartering; but what
of that? if it please the eye of one, it is with me as the
very true sonnet is, 'Please one, and please all.'

OLIVIA

Why, how dost thou, man? what is the matter with thee?

MALVOLIO

Not black in my mind, though yellow in my legs. It did
come to his hands, and commands shall be executed: I
think we do know the sweet Roman hand.

OLIVIA

Wilt thou go to bed, Malvolio?

MALVOLIO

To bed! ay, sweet-heart; and I'll come to thee.

OLIVIA

God comfort thee! Why dost thou smile so, and kiss thy
hand so oft?

MARIA

How do you, Malvolio?

MALVOLIO

At your request! yes; nightingales answer daws.

MARIA

Why appear you with this ridiculous boldness before my lady?

MALVOLIO

'Be not afraid of greatness': — 'twas well writ.

OLIVIA

What mean'st thou by that, Malvolio?

MALVOLIO

'Some are born great,' —

OLIVIA

Ha!

MALVOLIO

'Some achieve greatness,' —

OLIVIA

What say'st thou?

MALVOLIO

'And some have greatness thrust upon them.'

OLIVIA

Heaven restore thee!

MALVOLIO

'Remember who commended thy yellow stockings,' —

OLIVIA

Thy yellow stockings!

MALVOLIO

'And wish'd to see thee cross-garter'd.'

OLIVIA

Cross-garter'd!

MALVOLIO

'Go to, thou art made, if thou desirest to be so'; —

OLIVIA

Am I made?

MALVOLIO

'If not, let me see thee a servant still.'

OLIVIA

Why, this is very midsummer madness.

Enter a SERVANT.

SERVANT

Madam, the young gentleman of the Count Orsino's is
return'd: I could hardly entreat him back: he attends
your ladyship's pleasure.

OLIVIA

I'll come to him. [*Exit* SERVANT.] Good Maria, let
this fellow be look'd to. Where's my cousin Toby? Let
some of my people have a special care of him: I would
not have him miscarry for the half of my dowry.

[*Exeunt* OLIVIA *and* MARIA.

MALVOLIO

O, ho! do you come near me now? no worse man than
Sir Toby to look to me? This concurs directly with the
letter: she sends him on purpose, that I may appear
stubborn to him; for she incites me to that in the letter.
'Cast thy humble slough,' says she; 'be opposite with a
kinsman, surly with servants; let thy tongue tang with
arguments of state; put thyself into the trick of
singularity'; — and, consequently, sets down the
manner how; as, a sad face, a reverend carriage, a slow
tongue, in the habit of some sir of note, and so forth. I
have limed her; but it is Jove's doing, and Jove make me
thankful! And, when she went away now, 'Let this fellow
be look'd to': fellow! not Malvolio, nor after my degree,
but fellow. Why, every thing adheres together, that no
dram of a scruple, no scruple of a scruple, no obstacle,
no incredulous or unsafe circumstance — What can be
said? Nothing, that can be, can come between me and
the full prospect of my hopes. Well, Jove, not I, is the
doer of this, and he is to be thank'd.

Enter MARIA *with* SIR TOBY *and* FABIAN.

SIR TOBY

Which way is he, in the name of sanctity? If all the devils
of hell be drawn in little, and Legion himself possess'd
him, yet I'll speak to him.

FABIAN

Here he is, here he is. — How is't with you, sir? how is't with you, man?

MALVOLIO

Go off; I discard you: let me enjoy my private: go off.

MARIA

Lo, how hollow the fiend speaks within him; did not I tell you? — Sir Toby, my lady prays you to have a care of him.

MALVOLIO

Ah, ha! does she so?

MALVOLIO Go off; I discard you: let me enjoy my private: go off.

SIR TOBY

Go to, go to; peace, peace; we must deal gently with him: let me alone. — How do you, Malvolio? how is't with you? What, man! defy the devil: consider, he's an enemy to mankind.

MALVOLIO

Do you know what you say?

MARIA

La you, an you speak ill of the devil, how he takes it at heart! Pray God, he be not bewitch'd!

FABIAN

Carry his water to th'wise woman.

MARIA

Marry, and it shall be done to-morrow morning, if I live. My lady would not lose him for more than I'll say.

MALVOLIO

How now, mistress!

MARIA

O Lord!

SIR TOBY

Prithee, hold thy peace; this is not the way: do you not see you move him? let me alone with him.

FABIAN

No way but gentleness; gently, gently: the fiend is rough, and will not be roughly used.

SIR TOBY

Why, how now, my bawcock! how dost thou, chuck?

MALVOLIO

Sir!

SIR TOBY

Ay, Biddy, come with me. What, man! 'tis not for gravity to play at cherry-pit with Satan: hang him, foul collier!

MARIA

Get him to say his prayers; good Sir Toby; get him to pray.

MALVOLIO

My prayers, minx!

MARIA

No, I warrant you, he will not hear of godliness.

MALVOLIO

Go, hang yourselves all! you are idle shallow things: I am not of your element: you shall know more hereafter[*Exit.*

SIR TOBY

Is't possible?

FABIAN

If this were play'd upon a stage now, I could condemn it as an improbable fiction.

SIR TOBY

His very genius hath taken the infection of the device, man.

MARIA

Nay, pursue him now, lest the device take air, and taint.

FABIAN

Why, we shall make him mad indeed.

MARIA

The house will be the quieter.

SIR TOBY

Come, we'll have him in a dark room and bound. My niece is already in the belief that he's mad; we may carry it thus, for our pleasure and his penance, till our very pastime, tired out of breath, prompt us to have mercy on him: at which time we will bring the device to the bar, and crown thee for a finder of madmen. — But see, but see.

FABIAN

More matter for a May morning.

Enter SIR ANDREW.

SIR ANDREW

Here's the challenge, read it: warrant there's vinegar and pepper in't.

FABIAN

  Is't so saucy?

SIR ANDREW

  Ay, is't, I warrant him: do but read.

SIR TOBY

  Give me. [*reads*] Youth, whatsoever thou art, thou art
  but a scurvy fellow.

FABIAN

  Good, and valiant.

SIR TOBY [*reads*].

  Wonder not, nor admire not in thy mind, why I do call
  thee so, for I will show thee no reason for't.

FABIAN

  A good note: that keeps you from the blow of the law.

SIR TOBY [*reads*].

  Thou comest to the Lady Olivia, and in my sight she
  uses thee kindly: but thou liest in thy throat; that is not
  the matter I challenge thee for.

FABIAN

  Very brief, and to exceeding good sense — less.

SIR TOBY [*reads*].

  I will waylay thee going home; where if it be thy chance
  to kill me, —

FABIAN

  Good.

SIR TOBY [*reads*].

  Thou kill'st me like a rogue and a villain.

FABIAN

  Still you keep o'th'windy side of the law: good.

SIR TOBY [*reads*].

  Fare thee well; and God have mercy upon one of our
  souls! He may have mercy upon mine; but my hope is
  better, and so look to thyself. Thy friend, as thou usest
  him, and thy sworn enemy,

                    ANDREW AGUECHEEK.

If this letter move him not, his legs cannot: I'll give't him.

MARIA

You may have very fit occasion for't: he is now in some commerce with my lady, and will by and by depart.

SIR TOBY

Go, Sir Andrew; scout me for him at the corner of the orchard, like a bum-baily: so soon as ever thou seest him, draw; and, as thou draw'st, swear horrible; for it comes to pass oft, that a terrible oath, with a swaggering accent sharply twang'd off, gives manhood more approbation than ever proof itself would have earn'd him. Away!

SIR ANDREW

Nay, let me alone for swearing.   [*Exit.*

SIR TOBY

Now will not I deliver his letter: for the behaviour of the young gentleman gives him out to be of good capacity and breeding: his employment between his lord and my niece confirms no less: therefore this letter, being so excellently ignorant, will breed no terror in the youth: he will find it comes from a clodpole. But, sir, I will deliver his challenge by word of mouth; set upon Aguecheek a notable report of valour; and drive the gentleman — as I know his youth will aptly receive it — into a most hideous opinion of his rage, skill, fury, and impetuosity. This will so fright them both, that they will kill one another by the look, like cockatrices.

FABIAN

Here he comes with your niece: give them way till he take leave, and presently after him.

SIR TOBY

I will meditate the while upon some horrid message for a challenge.

[*Exeunt* SIR TOBY, FABIAN, *and* MARIA.
Enter OLIVIA, *with* VIOLA.

72

OLIVIA

I have said too much unto a heart of stone,
And laid mine honour too unchary out:
There's something in me that reproves my fault;
But such a headstrong potent fault it is,
That it but mocks reproof.

VIOLA

With the same 'haviour that your passion bears,
Goes on my master's griefs.

OLIVIA

Here, wear this jewel for me, 'tis my picture:
Refuse it not: it hath no tongue to vex you:
And, I beseech you, come again to-morrow.
What shall you ask of me that I'll deny,
That honour sav'd may upon asking give?

VIOLA

Nothing but this, — your true love for my master.

OLIVIA

How with mine honour may I give him that
Which I have given to you?

VIOLA

                    I will acquit you.

OLIVIA

Well, come again to-morrow; fare thee well:
A fiend like thee might bear my soul to hell.   [*Exit.*

Enter SIR TOBY *and* FABIAN.

SIR TOBY

Gentleman, God save thee!

VIOLA

And you, sir.

SIR TOBY

That defence thou hast, betake thee to't: of what nature
the wrongs are thou hast done him, I know not: but thy
intercepter, full of despite, bloody as the hunter, attends
thee at the orchard-end: dismount thy tuck, be yare in

73

thy preparation; for thy assailant is quick, skilful, and deadly.

VIOLA

You mistake, sir; I am sure no man hath any quarrel to me: my remembrance is very free and clear from any image of offence done to any man.

SIR TOBY

You'll find it otherwise, I assure you: therefore, if you hold your life at any price, betake you to your guard; for your opposite hath in him what youth, strength, skill, and wrath can furnish man withal.

VIOLA

I pray you, sir, what is he?

SIR TOBY

He is knight, dubb'd with unhatch'd rapier and on carpet consideration; but he is a devil in private brawl: souls and bodies hath he divorced three; and his incensement at this moment is so implacable, that satisfaction can be none but by pangs of death and sepulchre: hob-nob is his word; give't or take't.

VIOLA

I will return again into the house, and desire some conduct of the lady. I am no fighter. I have heard of some kind of men that put quarrels purposely on others, to taste their valour; belike this is a man of that quirk.

SIR TOBY

Sir, no; his indignation derives itself out of a very competent injury: therefore, get you on, and give him his desire. Back you shall not to the house, unless you undertake that with me which with as much safety you might answer him: therefore, on, or strip your sword stark naked; for meddle you must, that's certain, or forswear to wear iron about you.

VIOLA

This is as uncivil as strange. I beseech you, do me this courteous office, as to know of the knight what my

offence to him is: it is something of my negligence,
nothing of my purpose.

SIR TOBY

I will do so. — Signior Fabian, stay you by this gentleman
till my return. [*Exit.*

VIOLA

Pray you, sir, do you know of this matter?

FABIAN

I know the knight is incensed against you, even to a
mortal arbitrement; but nothing of the circumstance
more.

VIOLA

I beseech you, what manner of man is he?

FABIAN

Nothing of that wonderful promise, to read him by his
form, as you are like to find him in the proof of his
valour. He is, indeed, sir, the most skilful, bloody, and
fatal opposite that you could possibly have found in any
part of Illyria. Will you walk towards him? I will make
your peace with him, if I can.

VIOLA

I shall be much bound to you for't: I am one that had
rather go with sir priest than sir knight: I care not who
knows so much of my mettle. [*Exeunt.*

Enter SIR TOBY *and* SIR ANDREW.

SIR TOBY

Why, man, he's a very devil; I have not seen such a
firago. I had a pass with him, rapier, scabbard, and all,
and he gives me the stuck-in with such a mortal motion,
that it is inevitable; and on the answer, he pays you as
surely as your feet hit the ground they step on: they say
he has been fencer to the Sophy.

SIR ANDREW

Pox on't, I'll not meddle with him.

SIR TOBY

Ay, but he will not now be pacified: Fabian can scarce hold him yonder.

SIR ANDREW

Plague on't, an I thought he had been valiant and so cunning in fence, I'ld have seen him damn'd ere I'ld have challenged him. Let him let the matter slip, and I'll give him my horse, grey Capulet.

SIR TOBY

I'll make the motion: stand here, make a good show on't: this shall end without the perdition of souls. — [*aside*] Marry, I'll ride your horse as well as I ride you.

Enter FABIAN *and* VIOLA.

[*to* FABIAN] I have his horse to take up the quarrel: I have persuaded him the youth's a devil.

FABIAN

He is as horribly conceited of him; and pants and looks pale, as if a bear were at his heels.

SIR TOBY [*to* VIOLA].

There's no remedy, sir; he will fight with you for's oath-sake: marry, he hath better bethought him of his quarrel, and he finds that now scarce to be worth talking of: therefore draw, for the supportance of his vow; he protests he will not hurt you.

VIOLA [*aside*].

Pray God defend me! A little thing would make me tell them how much I lack of a man.

FABIAN

Give ground, if you see him furious.

SIR TOBY

Come, Sir Andrew, there's no remedy; the gentleman will, for his honour's sake, have one bout with you; he cannot by the duello avoid it: but he has promised me, as he is a gentleman and a soldier, he will not hurt you. Come on, to't.

SIR ANDREW

Pray God, he keep his oath!   [*Draws.*

VIOLA

I do assure you, 'tis against my will.   [*Draws.*

Enter ANTONIO.

ANTONIO

Put up your sword. If this young gentleman
Have done offence, I take the fault on me:
If you offend him, I for him defy you.

SIR TOBY

You, sir! why, what are you?

ANTONIO [*drawing*].

One, sir, that for his love dares yet do more
Than you have heard him brag to you he will.

SIR TOBY

Nay, if you be an undertaker, I am for you.   [*Draws.*

FABIAN

O good Sir Toby, hold! here come the officers.

SIR TOBY [*to* ANTONIO].

I'll be with you anon.

VIOLA [*to* ANTONIO].

Pray, sir, put your sword up, if you please.

SIR ANDREW

Marry, will I, sir; and, for that I promised you,
I'll be as good as my word: he will bear you easily, and
reins well.

Enter OFFICERS.

FIRST OFFICER

This is the man; do thy office.

SECOND OFFICER

Antonio, I arrest thee at the suit of Count Orsino.

ANTONIO

You do mistake me, sir.

FIRST OFFICER

No, sir, no jot; I know your favour well,
Though now you have no sea-cap on your head. —

Take him away: he knows I know him well.

ANTONIO

I must obey. [*to* VIOLA] This comes with seeking you:
But there's no remedy; I shall answer it.
What will you do, now my necessity
Makes me to ask you for my purse? It grieves me
Much more for what I cannot do for you
Than what befalls myself. You stand amazed;
But be of comfort.

SECOND OFFICER

            Come, sir, away.

ANTONIO

I must entreat of you some of that money.

VIOLA

What money, sir?
For the fair kindness you have show'd me here,
And, part, being prompted by your present trouble,
Out of my lean and low ability
I'll lend you something: my having is not much;
I'll make division of my present with you:
Hold, there's half my coffer.

ANTONIO

            Will you deny me now?
Is't possible that my deserts to you
Can lack persuasion? Do not tempt my misery,
Lest that it makes me so unsound a man
As to upbraid you with those kindnesses
That I have done for you.

VIOLA

            I know of none;
Nor know I you by voice or any feature:
I hate ingratitude more in a man
Than lying, vainness, babbling, drunkenness,
Or any taint of vice whose strong corruption
Inhabits our frail blood.

ANTONIO

            O heavens themselves!

SECOND OFFICER

Come, sir, I pray you, go.

ANTONIO

Let me speak a little. This youth that you see here
I snatch'd one half out of the jaws of death,
Reliev'd him with such sanctity of love,
And to his image, which methought did promise
Most venerable worth, did I devotion.

FIRST OFFICER

What's that to us? The time goes by: away!

ANTONIO

But, O, how vile an idol proves this god!
Thou hast, Sebastian, done good feature shame.
In nature there's no blemish but the mind;
None can be call'd deform'd but the unkind:
Virtue is beauty, but the beauteous evil
Are empty trunks, o'erflourish'd by the devil.

FIRST OFFICER

The man grows mad: away with him! — come, come, sir.

ANTONIO

Lead me on.   [*Exit with* OFFICERS.

VIOLA

Methinks his words do from such passion fly,
That he believes himself: so do not I.
Prove true, imagination, O, prove true,
That I, dear brother, be now ta'en for you!

SIR TOBY

Come hither, knight; come hither, Fabian: we'll whisper
o'er a couplet or two of most sage saws.

VIOLA

He nam'd Sebastian: I my brother know
Yet living in my glass; even such, and so,
In favour was my brother; and he went
Still in this fashion, colour, ornament, —
For him I imitate: O, if it prove,
Tempests are kind, and salt waves fresh in love!   [*Exit.*

79

SIR TOBY

A very dishonest paltry boy, and more a coward than a
hare: his dishonesty appears in leaving his friend here in
necessity, and denying him; and for his cowardship, ask
Fabian.

FABIAN

A coward, a most devout coward, religious in it.

SIR ANDREW

'Slid, I'll after him again, and beat him.

SIR TOBY

Do; cuff him soundly, but never draw thy sword.

SIR ANDREW

An I do not, — [*Exit.*

FABIAN

Come, let's see the event.

SIR TOBY

I dare lay any money 'twill be nothing yet. [*Exeunt.*

ACT IV

SCENE I

Before OLIVIA'S *house.*
Enter SEBASTIAN *and* CLOWN.

CLOWN

Will you make me believe that I am not sent for you?

SEBASTIAN

Go to, go to, thou art a foolish fellow:
Let me be clear of thee.

CLOWN

Well held out, i'faith! No, I do not know you; nor I am
not sent to you by my lady, to bid you come speak with
her; nor your name is not Master Cesario; nor this is not
my nose neither. Nothing that is so is so.

SEBASTIAN

I prithee, vent thy folly somewhere else;
Thou know'st not me.

CLOWN

Vent my folly! he has heard that word of some great
man, and now applies it to a fool: vent my folly! I am
afraid this great lubber, the world, will prove a cockney.
— I prithee, now, ungird thy strangeness, and tell me
what I shall vent to my lady: shall I vent to her that thou
art coming?

SEBASTIAN

I prithee, foolish Greek, depart from me:
There's money for thee: if you tarry longer,
I shall give worse payment.

CLOWN

By my troth, thou hast an open hand. — These wise
men, that give fools money, get themselves a good
report after fourteen years' purchase.

Enter SIR ANDREW.

SIR ANDREW

Now, sir, have I met you again? there's for you.

[*Striking* SEBASTIAN.

SEBASTIAN

Why, there's for thee, and there, and there!

[*Beating* SIR ANDREW.

Are all the people mad?

Enter SIR TOBY *and* FABIAN.

SEBASTIAN Why, there's for thee, and there, and there! Are all the people mad?.

SIR TOBY

Hold, sir, or I'll throw your dagger o'er the house.

CLOWN

This will I tell my lady straight: I would not be in some of
your coats for twopence.   [*Exit.*

SIR TOBY

Come on, sir; hold.

SIR ANDREW

Nay, let him alone: I'll go another way to work with
him: I'll have an action of battery against him, if there
be any law in Illyria: though I struck him first, yet it's no
matter for that.

SEBASTIAN

Let go thy hand.

SIR TOBY

Come, sir, I will not let you go. Come, my young
soldier, put up your iron: you are well flesh'd; come on.

SEBASTIAN

I will be free from thee. What wouldst thou now?
If thou darest tempt me further, draw thy sword. [*Draws.*

SIR TOBY

What, what? Nay, then I must have an ounce or two of
this malapert blood from you.   [*Draws.*

Enter OLIVIA.

OLIVIA

Hold, Toby; on thy life, I charge thee, hold!

SIR TOBY

Madam!

OLIVIA

Will it be ever thus? Ungracious wretch,
Fit for the mountains and the barbarous caves,
Where manners ne'er were preach'd! out of my sight! —
Be not offended, dear Cesario. —
Rudesby, be gone!

[*Exeunt* SIR TOBY, SIR ANDREW, *and* FABIAN.
I prithee, gentle friend,

Let thy fair wisdom, not thy passion, sway
In this uncivil and unjust extent
Against thy peace. Go with me to my house;
And hear thou there how many fruitless pranks
This ruffian hath botch'd up, that thou thereby
Mayst smile at this: thou shalt not choose but go:
Do not deny. Beshrew his soul for me,
He started one poor heart of mine in thee.

SEBASTIAN

What relish is in this? how runs the stream?
Or I am mad, or else this is a dream:
Let fancy still my sense in Lethe steep;
If it be thus to dream, still let me sleep!

OLIVIA

Nay, come, I prithee: would thou'ldst be rul'd by me!

SEBASTIAN

Madam, I will.

OLIVIA

O, say so, and so be! [*Exeunt.*

SCENE II

OLIVIA'S *house.*

Enter MARIA *and* CLOWN.

MARIA

Nay, I prithee, put on this gown and this beard; make him
believe thou art Sir Topas the curate: do it quickly; I'll call
Sir Toby the whilst. [*Exit.*

CLOWN

Well, I'll put it on, and I will dissemble myself in't; and
I would I were the first that ever dissembled in such a
gown. I am not tall enough to become the function well;
nor lean enough to be thought a good student: but to be
said an honest man and a good housekeeper, goes as
fairly as to say a careful man and a great scholar. The
competitors enter.

84

Enter SIR TOBY *and* MARIA.

SIR TOBY

Jove bless thee, master parson.

CLOWN

Bonos dies, Sir Toby: for, as the old hermit of Prague,
that never saw pen and ink, very wittily said to a niece of
King Gorboduc, 'That that is is'; so I, being master
parson, am master parson; for, what is that but that, and
is but is?

SIR TOBY

To him, Sir Topas.

CLOWN

What, ho, I say, — peace in this prison!

SIR TOBY

The knave counterfeits well; a good knave.

MALVOLIO [*within*].

Who calls there?

CLOWN

Sir Topas the curate, who comes to visit Malvolio the
lunatic.

MALVOLIO

Sir Topas, Sir Topas, good Sir Topas, go to my lady.

CLOWN

Out, hyperbolical fiend! how vexest thou this man!
talkest thou nothing but of ladies?

SIR TOBY

Well said, master parson.

MALVOLIO

Sir Topas, never was man thus wrong'd: good Sir
Topas, do not think I am mad: they have laid me here in
hideous darkness.

CLOWN

Fie, thou dishonest Satan! I call thee by the most
modest terms; for I am one of those gentle ones that will
use the devil himself with courtesy: say'st thou that
house is dark?

MALVOLIO

As hell, Sir Topas.

CLOWN

Why, it hath bay windows transparent as barricadoes, and the clearstories toward the south-north are as lustrous as ebony; and yet complainest thou of obstruction?

MALVOLIO

I am not mad, Sir Topas: I say to you, this house is dark.

CLOWN

Madman, thou errest: I say, there is no darkness but ignorance; in which thou art more puzzled than the Egyptians in their fog.

MALVOLIO

I say, this house is as dark as ignorance, though ignorance were as dark as hell; and I say, there was never man thus abused. I am no more mad than you are: make the trial of it in any constant question.

CLOWN

What is the opinion of Pythagoras concerning wildfowl?

MALVOLIO

That the soul of our grandam might haply inhabit a bird.

CLOWN

What think'st thou of his opinion?

MALVOLIO

I think nobly of the soul, and no way approve his opinion.

CLOWN

Fare thee well. Remain thou still in darkness: thou shalt hold the opinion of Pythagoras ere I will allow of thy wits; and fear to kill a woodcock, lest thou dispossess the soul of thy grandam. Fare thee well.

MALVOLIO

Sir Topas, Sir Topas, —

SIR TOBY

My most exquisite Sir Topas!

CLOWN

Nay, I am for all waters.

MARIA

Thou mightst have done this without thy beard and
gown: he sees thee not.

SIR TOBY

To him in thine own voice, and bring me word how thou
find'st him: I would we were well rid of this knavery. If he
may be conveniently deliver'd, I would he were; for I am
now so far in offence with my niece, that I cannot pursue
with any safety this sport to the upshot. Come by and by
to my chamber.   [*Exeunt* SIR TOBY *and* MARIA.

CLOWN [*singing*].

  Hey, Robin, jolly Robin,
   Tell me how thy lady does.

MALVOLIO

Fool, —

CLOWN

'My lady is unkind, perdy.'

MALVOLIO

Fool, —

CLOWN

'Alas, why is she so?'

MALVOLIO

Fool, I say, —

CLOWN

'She loves another' — Who calls, ha?

MALVOLIO

Good fool, as ever thou wilt deserve well at my hand,
help me to a candle, and pen, ink and paper: as I am a
gentleman, I will live to be thankful to thee for't.

CLOWN

Master Malvolio!

MALVOLIO
  Ay, good fool.

CLOWN
  Alas, sir, how fell you besides your five wits?

MALVOLIO
  Fool, there was never a man so notoriously abused:
  I am as well in my wits, fool, as thou art.

CLOWN
  But as well? then you are mad indeed, if you be no
  better in your wits than a fool.

MALVOLIO
  They have here propertied me; keep me in darkness,
  send ministers to me, asses, and do all they can to face
  me out of my wits.

CLOWN
  Advise you what you say; the minister is here. —
  Malvolio, Malvolio, thy wits the heavens restore!
  endeavour thyself to sleep, and leave thy vain bibble-
  babble.

MALVOLIO
  Sir Topas, —

CLOWN
  Maintain no words with him, good fellow. — Who, I,
  sir? not I, sir. God b'wi' you, good Sir Topas! — Marry,
  amen. — I will, sir, I will.

MALVOLIO
  Fool, fool, fool, I say, —

CLOWN
  Alas, sir, be patient. What say you sir? I am shent for
  speaking to you.

MALVOLIO
  Good fool, help me to some light and some paper:
  I tell thee, I am as well in my wits as any man in Illyria.

CLOWN
  Well-a-day, that you were, sir!

MALVOLIO

By this hand, I am. Good fool, some ink, paper, and
light; and convey what I will set down to my lady: it shall
advantage thee more than ever the bearing of letter did.

CLOWN

I will help you to't. But tell me true, are you not mad
indeed? or do you but counterfeit?

MALVOLIO

Believe me, I am not; I tell thee true.

CLOWN

Nay, I'll ne'er believe a madman till I see his brains. I
will fetch you light, and paper, and ink.

MALVOLIO

Fool, I'll requite it in the highest degree: I prithee, be gone.

CLOWN [*singing*].

> I am gone, sir;
>   And anon, sir,
> I'll be with you again,
>   In a trice,
> Like to the old Vice,
> Your need to sustain;
> Who, with dagger of lath,
> In his rage and his wrath,
>   Cries, ah, ha! to the devil:
> Like a mad lad,
> Pare thy nails, dad;
>   Adieu, goodman devil.   [*Exit.*

SCENE III

OLIVIA'S *garden.*

Enter SEBASTIAN.

SEBASTIAN

This is the air; that is the glorious sun;
This pearl she gave me, I do feel't and see't:
And though 'tis wonder that enwraps me thus,

Yet 'tis not madness. Where's Antonio, then?
I could not find him at the Elephant:
Yet there he was; and there I found this credit,
That he did range the town to seek me out.
His counsel now might do me golden service;
For though my soul disputes well with my sense,
That this may be some error, but no madness,
Yet doth this accident and flood of fortune
So far exceed all instance, all discourse,
That I am ready to distrust mine eyes,
And wrangle with my reason, that persuades me
To any other trust but that I am mad
Or else the lady's mad; yet, if 'twere so,
She could not sway her house, command her followers,
Take and give back affairs, and their dispatch,
With such a smooth, discreet, and stable bearing,
As I perceive she does: there's something in't
That is deceivable. But here the lady comes.

Enter OLIVIA *and a* PRIEST.

OLIVIA

Blame not this haste of mine. If you mean well,
Now go with me and with this holy man
Into the chantry by: there, before him,
And underneath that consecrated roof,
Plight me the full assurance of your faith;
That my most jealous and too doubtful soul
May live at peace: he shall conceal it,
Whiles you are willing it shall come to note,
What time we will our celebration keep
According to my birth. — What do you say?

SEBASTIAN

I'll follow this good man, and go with you;
And, having sworn truth, ever will be true.

OLIVIA

Then lead the way, good father; and heavens so shine,
That they may fairly note this act of mine!   [*Exeunt.*

ACT V

SCENE I

Before OLIVIA'S *house.*

Enter CLOWN *and* FABIAN.

FABIAN

Now, as thou lovest me, let me see his letter.

CLOWN

Good Master Fabian, grant me another request.

FABIAN

Any thing.

CLOWN

Do not desire to see this letter.

FABIAN

This is, to give a dog, and in recompense desire my dog again.

Enter DUKE, VIOLA, CURIO, *and* ATTENDANTS.

DUKE

Belong you to the Lady Olivia, friends?

CLOWN

Ay, sir; we are some of her trappings.

DUKE

I know thee well: how dost thou, my good fellow?

CLOWN

Truly, sir, the better for my foes, and the worse for my
friends.

DUKE

Just the contrary; the better for thy friends.

CLOWN

No, sir, the worse.

DUKE

How can that be?

CLOWN

Marry, sir, they praise me, and make an ass of me; now
my foes tell me plainly I am an ass: so that by my foes, sir,
I profit in the knowledge of myself; and by my friends I
am abused: so that, conclusions to be as kisses, if your
four negatives make your two affirmatives, why, then, the
worse for my friends, and the better for my foes.

DUKE

Why, this is excellent.

CLOWN

By my troth, sir, no; though it please you to be one of
my friends.

DUKE

Thou shalt not be the worse for me: there's gold.

[*Gives money.*

CLOWN

But that it would be double-dealing, sir, I would you
could make it another.

DUKE

O, you give me ill counsel.

CLOWN

Put your Grace in your pocket, sir, for this once, and let
your flesh and blood obey it.

DUKE

Well, I will be so much a sinner to be a double-dealer:
there's another.   [*Gives money.*

CLOWN

Primo, secundo, tertio, is a good play; and the old saying
is, the third pays for all: the *triplex,* sir, is a good tripping
measure; or the bells of Saint Bennet, sir, may put you
in mind, — one, two, three.

DUKE

You can fool no more money out of me at this throw: if
you will let your lady know I am here to speak with her,
and bring her along with you, it may awake my bounty
further.

CLOWN

Marry, sir, lullaby to your bounty till I come again. I go,
sir; but I would not have you to think that my desire of
having is the sin of covetousness: but, as you say, sir, let
your bounty take a nap, I will awake it anon.   [*Exit.*

VIOLA

Here comes the man, sir, that did rescue me.

Enter OFFICERS, *with* ANTONIO.

DUKE

That face of his I do remember well;
Yet, when I saw it last, it was besmear'd
As black as Vulcan in the smoke of war:
A bawbling vessel was he captain of,
For shallow draught and bulk unprizable;
With which such scatheful grapple did he make
With the most noble bottom of our fleet,
That very envy and the tongue of loss
Cried fame and honour on him. — What's the matter?

FIRST OFFICER

Orsino, this is that Antonio

That took the Phœnix and her fraught from Candy;
And this is he that did the Tiger board,
When your young nephew Titus lost his leg:
Here in the streets, desperate of shame and state,
In private brabble did we apprehend him.

VIOLA

He did me kindness, sir; drew on my side;
But, in conclusion, put strange speech upon me, —
I know not what 'twas but distraction.

DUKE

Notable pirate! thou salt-water thief!
What foolish boldness brought thee to their mercies,
Whom thou, in terms so bloody and so dear,
Hast made thine enemies?

ANTONIO

                    Orsino, noble sir,
Be pleas'd that I shake off these names you give me:
Antonio never yet was thief or pirate,
Though, I confess, on base and ground enough,
Orsino's enemy. A witchcraft drew me hither:
That most ingrateful boy there by your side,
From the rude sea's enrag'd and foamy mouth
Did I redeem; a wreck past hope he was:
His life I gave him, and did thereto add
My love, without retention or restraint,
All his in dedication; for his sake
Did I expose myself, pure for his love,
Into the danger of this adverse town;
Drew to defend him when he was beset:
Where being apprehended, his false cunning,
Not meaning to partake with me in danger,
Taught him to face me out of his acquaintance,
And grew a twenty-years-removed thing
While one would wink; denied me mine own purse,
Which I had recommended to his use
Not half an hour before.

VIOLA

How can this be?

DUKE

When came he to this town?

ANTONIO

To-day, my lord: and for three months before —
No interim, not a minute's vacancy —
Both day and night did we keep company.

DUKE

Here comes the countess: now heaven walks on earth. —
But for thee, fellow; fellow, thy words are madness:
Three months this youth hath tended upon me;
But more of that anon. Take him aside.

Enter OLIVIA *and* ATTENDANTS.

OLIVIA

What would my lord, but that he may not have,
Wherein Olivia may seem serviceable? —
Cesario, you do not keep promise with me.

VIOLA

Madam!

DUKE

Gracious Olivia, —

OLIVIA

What do you say, Cesario? Good my lord, —

VIOLA

My lord would speak; my duty hushes me.

OLIVIA

If it be aught to the old tune, my lord,
It is as fat and fulsome to mine ear
As howling after music.

DUKE

Still so cruel?

OLIVIA

Still so constant, lord.

DUKE
   What, to perverseness? you uncivil lady,
   To whose ingrate and inauspicious altars
   My soul the faithfull'st offerings hath breath'd out
   That e'er devotion tender'd! What shall I do?

OLIVIA
   Even what it please my lord, that shall become him.

DUKE
   Why should I not, had I the heart to do it,
   Like to th'Egyptian thief at point of death,
   Kill what I love? a savage jealousy
   That sometimes savours nobly. — But hear me this:
   Since you to non-regardance cast my faith,
   And that I partly know the instrument
   That screws me from my true place in your favour,
   Live you, the marble-breasted tyrant, still;
   But this your minion, whom I know you love,
   And whom, by heaven I swear, I tender dearly,
   Him will I tear out of that cruel eye,
   Where he sits crowned in his master's spite. —
   Come, boy, with me; my thoughts are ripe in mischief:
   I'll sacrifice the lamb that I do love,
   To spite a raven's heart within a dove.

VIOLA
   And I, most jocund, apt, and willingly,
   To do you rest, a thousand deaths would die.

OLIVIA
   Where goes Cesario?

VIOLA
                     After him I love
   More than I love these eyes, more than my life,
   More, by all mores, than e'er I shall love wife.
   If I do feign, you witnesses above
   Punish my life for tainting of my love!

OLIVIA
   Ay me, detested! how am I beguiled!

96

VIOLA

Who does beguile you? who does do you wrong?

OLIVIA

Hast thou forgot thyself? is it so long?
Call forth the holy father.   [*Exit an* ATTENDANT.

DUKE

Come, away!   [*To* VIOLA.

OLIVIA

Whither, my lord? — Cesario, husband, stay.

DUKE

Husband!

OLIVIA

Ay, husband: can he that deny?

DUKE

Her husband, sirrah!

VIOLA

No, my lord, not I.

OLIVIA

Alas, it is the baseness of thy fear
That makes thee strangle thy propriety:
Fear not, Cesario; take thy fortunes up;
Be that thou know'st thou art, and then thou art
As great as that thou fear'st.

Enter ATTENDANT, *with* PRIEST.

O, welcome, father!
Father, I charge thee, by thy reverence,
Here to unfold — though lately we intended
To keep in darkness what occasion now
Reveals before 'tis ripe — what thou dost know
Hath newly pass'd between this youth and me.

PRIEST

A contract of eternal bond of love,
Confirm'd by mutual joinder of your hands,
Attested by the holy close of lips,
Strengthen'd by interchangement of your rings;
And all the ceremony of this compact
Seal'd in my function, by my testimony:

97

Since when, my watch hath told me, toward my grave
I have travell'd but two hours.

DUKE

O thou dissembling cub! what wilt thou be
When time hath sow'd a grizzle on thy case?
Or will not else thy craft so quickly grow,
That thine own trip shall be thine overthrow?
Farewell, and take her; but direct thy feet
Where thou and I henceforth may never meet.

VIOLA

My lord, I do protest, —

OLIVIA

              O, do not swear!
Hold little faith, though thou hast too much fear.

          Enter SIR ANDREW.

SIR ANDREW

For the love of God, a surgeon! send one presently to
Sir Toby.

OLIVIA

What's the matter?

SIR ANDREW

'Has broke my head across, and has given Sir Toby a
bloody coxcomb too: for the love of God, your help! I
had rather than forty pound I were at home.

OLIVIA

Who has done this, Sir Andrew?

SIR ANDREW

The count's gentleman, one Cesario: we took him for a
coward, but he's the very devil incardinate.

DUKE

My gentleman Cesario?

SIR ANDREW

'Od's lifelings, here he is! — You broke my head for
nothing; and that that I did, I was set on to do't by Sir
Toby.

VIOLA

Why do you speak to me? I never hurt you:
You drew your sword upon me without cause;
But I bespake you fair, and hurt you not.

SIR ANDREW

If a bloody coxcomb be a hurt, you have hurt me: I
think you set nothing by a bloody coxcomb. — Here
comes Sir Toby halting; you shall hear more: but if he
had not been in drink, he would have tickled you
othergates than he did.

Enter SIR TOBY and CLOWN.

DUKE

How now, gentleman! how is't with you?

SIR TOBY

That's all one: 'has hurt me, and there's the end on't. —
Sot, didst see Dick surgeon, sot?

CLOWN

O, he's drunk, Sir Toby, an hour agone; his eyes were
set at eight i'th'morning.

SIR TOBY

Then he's a rogue and a passy-measures pavin: I hate a
drunken rogue.

OLIVIA

Away with him! Who hath made this havoc with them?

SIR ANDREW

I'll help you, Sir Toby, because we'll be dress'd
together.

SIR TOBY

Will you help? an ass-head and a coxcomb and a knave,
a thin-faced knave, a gull?

OLIVIA

Get him to bed, and let his hurt be look'd to.

[*Exeunt* CLOWN, FABIAN, SIR TOBY, *and* SIR
ANDREW.

Enter SEBASTIAN.

99

SEBASTIAN

I am sorry, madam, I have hurt your kinsman;
But, had it been the brother of my blood,
I must have done no less with wit and safety.
You throw a strange regard upon me, and by that
I do perceive it hath offended you:
Pardon me, sweet one, even for the vows
We made each other but so late ago.

DUKE

One face, one voice, one habit, and two persons, —
A natural perspective, that is and is not!

SEBASTIAN

Antonio, O my dear Antonio!
How have the hours rack'd and tortured me,
Since I have lost thee!

ANTONIO

Sebastian are you?

SEBASTIAN

               Fear'st thou that, Antonio?

ANTONIO

How have you made division of yourself?
An apple, cleft in two, is not more twin
Than these two creatures. Which is Sebastian?

OLIVIA

Most wonderful!

SEBASTIAN

Do I stand there? I never had a brother;
Nor can there be that deity in my nature,
Of here and every where. I had a sister,
Whom the blind waves and surges have devour'd. —
Of charity, what kin are you to me?   [*To* VIOLA.
What countryman? what name? what parentage?

VIOLA

Of Messaline: Sebastian was my father;
Such a Sebastian was my brother too,
So went he suited to his watery tomb:
If spirits can assume both form and suit,

You come to fright us.

SEBASTIAN

           A spirit I am indeed;
But am in that dimension grossly clad,
Which from the womb I did participate.
Were you a woman, as the rest goes even,
I should my tears let fall upon your cheek,
And say, 'Thrice-welcome, drowned Viola!'

VIOLA

My father had a mole upon his brow, —

SEBASTIAN

And so had mine.

VIOLA

And died that day when Viola from her birth
Had number'd thirteen years.

SEBASTIAN

O, that record is lively in my soul!
He finished, indeed, his mortal act
That day that made my sister thirteen years.

VIOLA

If nothing lets to make us happy both
But this my masculine usurp'd attire,
Do not embrace me till each circumstance
Of place, time, fortune, do cohere and jump,
That I am Viola: which to confirm,
I'll bring you to a captain in this town,
Where lie my maiden weeds; by whose gentle help
I was preserv'd to serve this noble count.
All the occurrence of my fortune since
Hath been between this lady and this lord.

SEBASTIAN [to OLIVIA].

So comes it, lady, you have been mistook:
But nature to her bias drew in that.
You would have been contracted to a maid;
Nor are you therein, by my life, deceived, —
You are betrothed both to a maid and man.

DUKE

Be not amaz'd; right noble is his blood. —
If this be so, as yet the glass seems true,
I shall have share in this most happy wrack. —
[to VIOLA] Boy, thou hast said to me a thousand times
Thou never shouldst love woman like to me.

VIOLA

And all those sayings will I over-swear;
And all those swearings keep as true in soul
As doth that orbed continent the fire
That severs day from night.

DUKE

Give me thy hand;
And let me see thee in thy woman's weeds.

VIOLA

The captain that did bring me first on shore
Hath my maid's garments: he, upon some action,
Is now in durance, at Malvolio's suit,
A gentleman and follower of my lady's.

OLIVIA

He shall enlarge him: — fetch Malvolio hither: —
And yet, alas, now I remember me,
They say, poor gentleman, he's much distract.

Enter CLOWN *with a letter, and* FABIAN.

A most extracting frenzy of mine own
From my remembrance clearly banish'd his. —
How does he, sirrah?

CLOWN

Truly, madam, he holds Beelzebub at the stave's end as
well as a man in his case may do: has here writ a letter to
you; I should have given't you to-day morning, but as a
madman's epistles are no gospels, so it skills not much
when they are deliver'd.

OLIVIA

Open't, and read it.

CLOWN

Look, then, to be well edified when the fool delivers the madman. [*reads*] By the Lord, madam, —

OLIVIA

How now! art thou mad?

CLOWN

No, madam, I do but read madness: an your ladyship will have it as it ought to be, you must allow *vox*.

OLIVIA

Prithee, read i' thy right wits.

CLOWN

So I do, madonna; but to read his right wits is to read thus: therefore perpend, my princess, and give ear.

OLIVIA

Read it you, sirrah.   [*to* FABIAN.

FABIAN [*reads*].

By the Lord, madam, you wrong me, and the world shall know it: though you have put me into darkness, and given your drunken cousin rule over me, yet have I the benefit of my senses as well as your ladyship. I have your own letter that induced me to the semblance I put on; with the which I doubt not but to do myself much right, or you much shame. Think of me as you please. I leave my duty a little unthought of, and speak out of my injury.

THE MADLY-USED MALVOLIO.

OLIVIA

Did he write this?

CLOWN

Ay, madam.

DUKE

This savours not much of distraction.

OLIVIA

See him deliver'd, Fabian; bring him hither.

[*Exit* FABIAN.

My lord, so please you, these things further thought on,

To think me as well a sister as a wife,
One day shall crown th'alliance on't, so please you,
Here at my house, and at my proper cost.

DUKE

Madam, I am most apt t'embrace your offer. —
[*to* VIOLA] Your master quits you; and, for your
    service done him,
So much against the mettle of your sex,
So far beneath your soft and tender breeding,
And since you call'd me master for so long,
Here is my hand: you shall from this time be
Your master's mistress.

OLIVIA

                            A sister! — you are she.

                Enter FABIAN, *with* MALVOLIO.

DUKE

Is this the madman?

OLIVIA

                            Ay, my lord, this same. —
How now, Malvolio!

MALVOLIO

                            Madam, you have done me wrong,
Notorious wrong.

OLIVIA

                    Have I, Malvolio? no.

MALVOLIO

Lady, you have. Pray you, peruse that letter:
You must not now deny it is your hand, —
Write from it, if you can, in hand or phrase;
Or say 'tis not your seal, nor your invention:
You can say none of this: well, grant it then,
And tell me, in the modesty of honour,
Why you have given me such clear lights of favour,
Bade me come smiling and cross-garter'd to you,
To put on yellow stockings, and to frown
Upon Sir Toby and the lighter people;

And, acting this in an obedient hope,
Why have you suffer'd me to be imprison'd,
Kept in a dark house, visited by the priest,
And made the most notorious geck and gull
That e'er invention play'd on? tell me why.

OLIVIA

Alas, Malvolio, this is not my writing,
Though, I confess, much like the character:
But, out of question, 'tis Maria's hand.
And now I do bethink me, it was she
First told me thou wast mad: thou camest in
    smiling,
And in such forms which here were presupposed
Upon thee in the letter. Prithee, be content:
This practice hath most shrewdly pass'd upon
    thee;
But, when we know the grounds and authors of it,
Thou shalt be both the plaintiff and the judge
Of thine own cause.

FABIAN

                    Good madam, hear me speak:
And let no quarrel nor no brawl to come
Taint the condition of this present hour,
Which I have wonder'd at. In hope it shall not,
Most freely I confess, myself and Toby
Set this device against Malvolio here,
Upon some stubborn and uncourteous parts
We had conceiv'd in him: Maria writ
The letter at Sir Toby's great importance;
In recompense whereof he hath married her.
How with a sportful malice it was follow'd,
May rather pluck on laughter than revenge;
If that the injuries be justly weigh'd
That have on both sides passed.

OLIVIA

Alas, poor fool, how have they baffled thee!

CLOWN

Why, 'some are born great, some achieve greatness, and
some have greatness thrown upon them.' I was one, sir,
in this interlude, — one Sir Topas, sir; but that's all one.
— 'By the Lord, fool, I am not mad'; — but do you
remember? 'Madam, why laugh you at such a barren
rascal? an you smile not, he's gagg'd': and thus the
whirligig of time brings in his revenges.

MALVOLIO

I'll be revenged on the whole pack of you. [*Exit.*

OLIVIA

He hath been most notoriously abused.

DUKE

Pursue him, and entreat him to a peace: —
He hath not told us of the captain yet:
When that is known, and golden time convents,
A solemn combination shall be made
Of our dear souls. Meantime, sweet sister,
We will not part from hence. — Cesario, come;
For so you shall be, while you are a man;
But when in other habits you are seen,
Orsino's mistress and his fancy's queen.

[*Exeunt all, except* CLOWN.

CLOWN [*sings*].

When that I was and a little tiny boy,
 With hey, ho, the wind and the rain,
A foolish thing was but a toy,
 For the rain it raineth every day.

But when I came to man's estate,
 With hey, ho, the wind and the rain,
'Gainst knaves and thieves men shut their gate,
 For the rain it raineth every day.

But when I came, alas! to wive,
 With hey, ho, the wind and the rain,
By swaggering could I never thrive,
 For the rain it raineth every day.

But when I came unto my beds,
    With hey, ho, the wind and the rain,
With toss-pots still had drunken heads,
    For the rain it raineth every day.

A great while ago the world begun,
    With hey, ho, the wind and the rain: —
But that's all one, our play is done,
    And we'll strive to please you every day. [*Exit.*

GLOSSARY

References are given only for words having more than one meaning, the first use of each sense being then noted.

Abate, *v.t.* to diminish. M.N.D. III. 2. 432. Deduct, except.
L.L.L. v. 2. 539. Cast down. Cor. III. 3. 134. Blunt. R III.
v. 5. 35. Deprive. Lear, II. 4. 159.

Abatement, *sb.* diminution Lear, I. 4. 59. Depreciation.
Tw.N. I. 1. 13.

Abjects, *sb.* outcasts, servile persons.

Able, *v.t.* to warrant.

Abode, *v.t.* to forebode. 3 H VI. V. 6. 45.

Abode, *sb.* stay, delay. M. of V. II. 6. 77.

Abodements, *sb.* forebodings.

Abram, *adj.* auburn.

Abridgement, *sb.* short entertainment, for pastime.

Abrook, *v.t.* to brook, endure.

Absey book, *sb.* ABC book, or primer.

Absolute, *adj.* resolved. M. for M. III. 1. 5. Positive. Cor.
III. 2. 39. Perfect. H V. III. 7. 26. Complete. Tp. I. 2. 109;
Lucr. 853.

Aby, *v.t.* to atone for, expiate.

Accite, *v.t.* to cite, summon.

Acknown, *adj.* cognisant.

Acture, *sb.* performance.

Addition, *sb.* title, attribute.

Adoptious, *adj.* given by adoption.

Advice, *sb.* consideration.

Aery, *sb.* eagle's nest or brood. R III. I. 3. 265, 271. Hence
generally any brood. Ham. II. 2. 344.

Affectioned, *p.p.* affected.

Affeered, *p.p.* sanctioned, confirmed.

Affiance, *sb.* confidence, trust.

Affined, *p.p.* related. T. & C. I. 3. 25. Bound. Oth. I. 1. 39.

Affront, *v.t.* to confront, meet.

Affy, *v.t.* to betroth. 2 H VI. IV. 1. 80. *v.t.* to trust. T.A. I.1. 47.

Aglet-baby, *sb.* small figure cut on the tag of a lace (Fr. *aiguillette*). T. of S. I. 2. 78.

Agnize, *v.t.* to acknowledge, confess.

Agood, *adv.* much.

Aim, *sb.* a guess.

Aim, to cry aim, to encourage, an archery term.

Alderliefest, *adj.* most loved of all.

Ale, *sb.* alehouse.

All amort, completely dejected (Fr. *a la mort*).

Allicholy, *sb.* melancholy.

Allow, *v.t.* to approve.

Allowance, *sb.* acknowledgement, approval.

Ames-ace, *sb.* the lowest throw of the dice.

Anchor, *sb.* anchorite, hermit.

Ancient, *sb.* ensign, standard. 1 H IV. IV. 2. 32. Ensign, ensign-bearer. 1 H IV. IV. 2. 24.

Ancientry, *sb.* antiquity, used of old people, W.T. III. 3. 62. Of the gravity which belongs to antiquity, M.A. II. 1. 75.

Angel, *sb.* gold coin, worth about 10s.

Antic, *adj.* fantastic. Ham. I. 5. 172.

Antick, *v.t.* to make a buffoon of. A. & C. II. 7. 126.

Antick, *sb.* buffoon of the old plays.

Appeal, *sb.* impeachment.

Appeal, *v.t.* to impeach.

Apperil, *sb.* peril.

Apple-john, *sb.* a shrivelled winter apple.

Argal, corruption of the Latin *ergo*, therefore.

Argo, corruption of *ergo*, therefore.

Aroint thee, begone, get thee gone.

Articulate, *v.i.* to make articles of peace. Cor. I. 9. 75. *v.t.* to set forth in detail. 1 H IV. V. 1. 72.

Artificial, *adj.* working by art.

Askance, *v.t.* to make look askance or sideways, make to avert.

Aspic, *sb.* asp.

Assured, *p.p.* betrothed.

Atone, *v.t.* to reconcile. R II. I. 1. 202. Agree. As V. 4. 112.

Attorney, *sb*. proxy, agent.

Attorneyed, *p.p.* done by proxy. W T. I. 1. 28. Engaged as an attorney, M. for M. V. 1. 383.

Attribute, *sb*. reputation.

Avail, *sb*. profit.

Avise, *v.t.* to inform. Are you avised? = Do you know?

Awful, *adj*. filled with regard for authority.

Awkward, *adj*. contrary.

Baby, *sb*. a doll.

Baccare, go back, a spurious Latin word.

Back-trick, a caper backwards in dancing.

Baffle, *v.t.* to disgrace (a recreant knight).

Bale, *sb*. evil, mischief.

Ballow, *sb*. cudgel.

Ban, *v.t.* curse. 2 H VI. II. 4. 25. *sb*. a curse. Ham. III. 2. 269.

Band, *sb*. bond.

Bank, *v.t.* sail along the banks of.

Bare, *v.t.* to shave.

Barn, *v.t.* to put in a barn.

Barn, or Barne, *sb*. bairn, child.

Base, *sb*. a rustic game. Bid the base = Challenge to a race. Two G. I. 2. 97.

Bases, *sb*. knee-length skirts worn by mounted knights.

Basilisco-like, Basilisco, a character in the play of *Soliman and Perseda*.

Basilisk, *sb*. a fabulous serpent. H V. V. 2. 17. A large cannon. 1 H IV. II. 3. 57.

Bate, *sb*. strife.

Bate, *v.i.* flutter as a hawk. 1 H IV. IV. 1. 99. Diminish. 1 H IV. III. 3. 2.

Bate, *v.t.* abate. Tp. I. 2. 250. Beat down, weaken. M. of V. III. 3. 32.

Bavin, *adj*. made of bavin or brushwood. 1 H IV. III. 2. 61.

Bawbling, *adj*. trifling, insignificant.

Baw-cock, *sb*. fine fellow (Fr. *beau coq*.) H V. III. 2. 25.

Bay, *sb*. space between the main timbers in a roof.

Beadsman, *sb.* one who is hired to offer prayers for another.

Bearing-cloth, *sb.* the cloth in which a child was carried to be christened.

Bear in hand, to deceive with false hopes.

Beat, *v.i.* to meditate. 2 H IV. II. 1. 20. Throb. Lear, III. 4. 14.

Becoming, *sb.* grace.

Beetle, *sb.* a heavy mallet, 2 H IV. I. 2. 235. Beetle-headed = heavy, stupid. T. of S. IV. 1. 150.

Behave, *v.t.* to control.

Behest, *sb.* command.

Behove, *sb.* behoof.

Be-lee'd, *p.p.* forced to lee of the wind.

Bench, *v.i.* to seat on the bench of justice. Lear, III. 6. 38. *v.t.* to elevate to the bench. W.T. I .2. 313.

Bench-hole, the hole of a privy.

Bergomask, a rustic dance, named from Bergamo in Italy.

Beshrew, *v.t.* to curse; but not used seriously.

Besort, *v.t.* to fit, suit.

Bestraught, *adj.* distraught.

Beteem, *v.t.* to permit, grant.

Bezonian, *sb.* a base and needy fellow.

Bias, *adj.* curving like the bias side of a bowling bowl.

Biggen, *sb.* a nightcap.

Bilbo, *sb.* a Spanish rapier, named from Bilbao or Bilboa.

Bilboes, *sb.* stocks used for punishment on shipboard.

Birdbolt, *sb.* a blunt-headed arrow used for birds.

Bisson, *adj.* dim-sighted. Cor. II. 1. 65. Bisson rheum = blinding tears. Ham. II. 2. 514.

Blacks, *sb.* black mourning clothes.

Blank, *sb.* the white mark in the centre of a target.

Blank, *v.t.* to blanch, make pale.

Blanks, *sb.* royal charters left blank to be filled in as occasion dictated.

Blench, *sb.* a swerve, inconsistency.

Blistered, *adj.* padded out, puffed.

Block, *sb.* the wood on which hats are made. M.A. I. 1. 71. Hence, the style of hat. Lear, IV. 6. 185.

Blood-boltered, *adj.* clotted with blood.

Blowse, *sb.* a coarse beauty.

Bob, *sb.* smart rap, jest.

Bob, *v.t.* to beat hard, thwack. R III. V. 3. 335. To obtain by fraud, cheat. T. & C. III. 1. 69.

Bodge, *v.i.* to budge.

Bodkin, *sb.* small dagger, stiletto.

Boggle, *v.i.* to swerve, shy, hesitate.

Boggler, *sb.* swerver.

Boln, *adj.* swollen.

Bolt, *v.t.* to sift, refine.

Bolter, *sb.* a sieve.

Bombard, *sb.* a leathern vessel for liquor.

Bona-robas, *sb.* flashily dressed women of easy virtue.

Bonnet, *v.i.* to doff the hat, be courteous.

Boot, *sb.* profit. 1 H VI. IV. 6. 52. That which is given over and above. R III. IV. 4. 65. Booty. 3 H VI. IV. 1. 13.

Boots, *sb.* Give me not the boots = do not inflict on me the torture of the boots, which were employed to wring confessions.

Bosky, *adj.* woody.

Botcher, *sb.* patcher of old clothes.

Bots, *sb.* small worms in horses.

Bottled, *adj.* big-bellied.

Brabble, *sb.* quarrel, brawl.

Brabbler, *sb.* a brawler.

Brach, *sb.* a hound-bitch.

Braid, *adj.* deceitful.

Braid, *v.t.* to upbraid, reproach.

Brain, *v.t.* to conceive in the brain.

Brazed, *p.p.* made like brass, perhaps hardened in the fire.

Breeched, *p.p.* as though wearing breeches. Mac. II. 3. 120.

Breeching, *adj.* liable to be breeched for a flogging.

Breese, *sb.* a gadfly.

Brib'd-buck, *sb.* perhaps a buck distributed in presents.

Brock, *sb.* badger.

Broken, *adj.* of a mouth with some teeth missing.

Broker, *sb.* agent, go-between.

Brownist, a follower of Robert Brown, the founder of the sect of Independents.

Buck, *v.t.* to wash and beat linen.

Buck-basket, *sb.* a basket to take linen to be bucked.

Bucking, *sb.* washing.

Buckle, *v.i.* to encounter hand to hand, cope. 1 H VI. I. 2. 95. To bow. 2 H VI. I. 1. 141.

Budget, *sb.* a leather scrip or bag.

Bug, *sb.* bugbear, a thing causing terror.

Bugle, *sb.* a black bead.

Bully, *sb.* a fine fellow.

Bully-rook, *sb.* a swaggering cheater.

Bung, *sb.* pickpocket.

Burgonet, *sb.* close-fitting Burgundian helmet.

Busky, *adj.* woody.

By-drinkings, *sb.* drinks taken between meals.

Caddis, *sb.* worsted trimming, galloon.

Cade, *sb.* cask, barrel.

Caitiff, *sb.* captive, slave, a wretch. *adj.* R II. I. 2. 53.

Caliver, *sb.* musket.

Callet, *sb.* trull, drab.

Calling, *sb.* appellation.

Calm, *sb.* qualm.

Canaries = quandary.

Canary, *sb.* a lively Spanish dance. *v.i.* to dance canary.

Canker, *sb.* the dog-rose or wild-rose. 1 H IV. I. 3. 176. A worm that destroys blossoms. M.N.D. II. 2.3.

Canstick, *sb.* candlestick.

Cantle, *sb.* piece, slice.

Canton, *sb.* canto.

Canvass, *v.t.* shake as in a sieve, take to task.

Capable, *adj.* sensible. As III. 5. 23. Sensitive, susceptible. Ham. III. 4. 128. Comprehensive. Oth. III. 3. 459. Able to possess. Lear, II. 1. 85.

Capocchia, *sb.* the feminine of capocchio (Ital.), simpleton.

Capriccio, *sb.* caprice, fancy.

Captious, *adj.* either a contraction of capacious or a coined word meaning capable of receiving.

Carack, *sb.* a large merchant ship.

Carbonado, *sb.* meat scotched for boiling. *v.t.* to hack like a carbonado.

Card, *sb.* a cooling card = a sudden and decisive stroke.

Card, *v.t.* to mix (liquids).

Cardecu, *sb.* quarter of a French crown (*quart d'écu*).

Care, *v.i.* to take care.

Careire, career, *sb.* a short gallop at full speed.

Carlot, *sb.* peasant.

Carpet consideration, On, used of those made knights for court services, not for valour in the field.

Carpet-mongers, *sb.* carpet-knights.

Carpets, *sb.* tablecloths.

Case, *v.t.* to strip off the case or skin of an animal. A.W. III. 6. 103. Put on a mask. 1 H IV. II. 2. 55.

Case, *sb.* skin of an animal. Tw.N. V. 1.163. A set, as of musical instruments, which were in fours. H V. III. 2. 4.

Cashiered, *p.p.* discarded; in M.W.W. I. 1. 168 it probably means relieved of his cash.

Cataian, *sb.* a native of Cathay, a Chinaman; a cant word.

Cater-cousins, good friends.

Catlings, *sb.* catgut strings for musical instruments.

Cautel, *sb.* craft, deceit, stratagem.

Cautelous, *adj.* crafty, deceitful.

Ceased, *p.p.* put off.

Censure, *sb.* opinion, judgement.

Certify, *v.t.* to inform, make certain.

Cess, *sb.* reckoning; out of all cess = immoderately.

Cesse = cease.

Champain, *sb.* open country.

Channel, *sb.* gutter.

Chape, *sb.* metal end of a scabbard.

Chapless, *adj.* without jaws.

Charact, *sb.* a special mark or sign of office.

Chare, *sb.* a turn of work.

Charge, *sb.* weight, importance. W.T. IV. 3. 258. Cost, expense. John I. 1. 49.

Chaudron, *sb.* entrails.

Check, *sb.* rebuke, reproof.

Check, *v.t.* to rebuke, chide.

Check, *v.i.* to start on sighting game.

Cherry-pit, *sb.* a childish game consisting of pitching cherry-stones into a small hole.

Cheveril, *sb.* leather of kid skin. R. & J. II. 3. 85. *adj.* Tw.N. III. 1. 12.

Che vor ye = I warn you.

Chewet, *sb.* chough. 1 H IV. V. 1. 29. (Fr. *chouette* or *chutte*). Perhaps with play on other meaning of chewet, *i.e.*, a kind of meat pie.

Childing, *adj.* fruitful.

Chop, *v.t.* to clop, pop.

Chopine, *sb.* shoe with a high sole.

Choppy, *adj.* chapped.

Christendom, *sb.* Christian name.

Chuck, *sb.* chick, term of endearment.

Chuff, *sb.* churl, boor.

Cinque pace, *sb.* a slow stately dance. M.A. II. 1. 72. Compare sink-a-pace in Tw.N. I. 3. 126.

Cipher, *v.t.* to decipher.

Circumstance, *sb.* particulars, details. Two G. I. 1. 36. Ceremonious phrases. M. of V. I. 1. 154.

Circumstanced, *p.p.* swayed by circumstance.

Citizen, *adj.* town-bred, effeminate.

Cittern, *sb.* guitar.

Clack-dish, *sb.* wooden dish carried by beggars.

Clamour, *v.t.* to silence.

Clapper-claw, *v.t.* to thrash, drub.

Claw, *v.t.* to scratch, flatter.

Clepe, *v.t.* to call.

Cliff, *sb.* clef, the key in music.

Cling, *v.t.* to make shrivel up.

Clinquant, *adj.* glittering with gold or silver lace or decorations.

Close, *sb.* cadence in music. R II. II. 1. 12. *adj.* secret. T. of S. Ind. I. 127. *v.i.* to come to an agreement, make terms. Two G. II. 5. 12.

Closely, *adv.* secretly.

Clout, *sb.* bull's-eye of a target.

Clouted, *adj.* hobnailed (others explain as patched).

Cobloaf, *sb.* a crusty, ill-shapen loaf.

Cockered, *p.p.* pampered.

Cockle, *sb.* the corncockle weed.

Cockney, *sb.* a city-bred person, a foolish wanton.

Cock-shut time, *sb.* twilight.

Codding, *adj.* lascivious.

Codling, *sb.* an unripe apple.

Cog, *v.i.* to cheat. R III I. 3. 48. *v.t.* to get by cheating, filch. Cor. III. 2. 133.

Coistrel, *sb.* groom.

Collection, *sb.* inference.

Collied, *p.p.* blackened, darkened.

Colour, *sb.* pretext. Show no colour, or bear no colour = allow of no excuse.

Colours, fear no colours = fear no enemy, be afraid of nothing.

Colt, *v.t.* to make a fool of, gull.

Combinate, *adj.* betrothed.

Combine, *v.t.* to bind.

Comfect, *sb.* comfit.

Commodity, *sb.* interest, advantage. John, II. 1. 573. Cargo of merchandise. Tw.N. III. 1. 46.

Comparative, *adj.* fertile in comparisons. 1 H IV. I. 2. 83.

Comparative, *sb.* a rival in wit. 1 H IV. III. 2. 67.

Compassed, *adj.* arched, round.

Complexion, *sb.* temperament.

Comply, *v.i.* to be ceremonious.

Composition, *sb.* agreement, consistency.

Composture, *sb.* compost.

Composure, *sb.* composition. T. & C. II. 3. 238; A. & C. I. 4. 22. Compact. T. & C. II. 3. 100.

Compt. *sb.* account, reckoning.

Comptible, *adj.* susceptible, sensitive.

Con, *v.t.* to study, learn; con thanks = give thanks.

Conceptious, *adj.* apt at conceiving.

Conclusion, *sb.* experiment.

Condolement, *sb.* lamentation. Ham. I. 2. 93. Consolation, Per. II. 1. 150.

Conduce, *v.i.* perhaps to tend to happen.

Conduct, *sb.* guide, escort.

Confiners, *sb.* border peoples.

Confound, *v.t.* to waste. 1 H IV. IV. 1. 3. 100. Destroy. M. of V. III. 2. 278.

Congied, *p.p.* taken leave (Fr. *congé*).

Consent, *sb.* agreement, plot.

Consist, *v.i.* to insist.

Consort, *sb.* company, fellowship. Two G. III. 2. 84; IV. 1. 64. *v.t.* to accompany. C. of E. I. 2. 28.

Conspectuity, *sb.* power of vision.

Constant, *adj.* consistent.

Constantly, *adv.* firmly, surely.

Conster, *v.t.* to construe, interpret.

Constringed, *p.p.* compressed.

Consul, *sb.* senator.

Containing, *sb.* contents.

Contraction, *sb.* the making of the marriage-contract.

Contrive, *v.t.* to wear out, spend. T. of S. I. 2. 273. Conspire. J.C. II. 3. 16.

Control, *v.t.* to check, contradict.

Convent, *v.t.* to summon.

Convert, *v.i.* to change.

Convertite, *sb.* a penitent.

Convince, *v.t.* to overcome. Mac. I. 7. 64. Convict. T. & C. II. 2. 130.

Convive, *v.i.* to banquet together.

Convoy, *sb.* conveyance, escort.

Copatain hat, *sb.* a high-crowned hat.

Cope, *v.t.* to requite. M. of V. IV. I. 412.

Copesmate, *sb.* a companion.

Copped, *adj.* round-topped.

Copulatives, *sb.* persons desiring to be coupled in marriage.

Copy, *sb.* theme, text. C. of E. V. I. 62. Tenure. Mac. III. 2. 37.

Coranto, *sb.* a quick, lively dance.

Corky, *adj.* shrivelled (with age).

Cornet, *sb.* a band of cavalry.

Corollary, *sb.* a supernumerary.

Cosier, *sb.* botcher, cobbler.

Costard, *sb.* an apple, the head (slang).

Cote, *v.t.* to come up with, pass on the way.

Cot-quean, *sb.* a man who busies himself in women's affairs.

Couch, *v.t.* to make to cower.

Counter, *adv.* to run or hunt counter is to trace the scent of the game backwards.

Counter, *sb.* a metal disk used in reckoning.

Counter-caster, *sb.* one who reckons by casting up counters.

Countermand, *v.t.* to prohibit, keep in check. C. of E. IV. 2. 37. Contradict. Lucr. 276.

Countervail, *v.t.* to outweigh.

County, *sb.* count. As II. 1. 67.

Couplet, *sb.* a pair.

Courser's hair, a horse's hair laid in water was believed to turn into a serpent.

Court holy-water, *sb.* flattery.

Courtship, *sb.* courtly manners.

Convent, *sb.* a convent.

Cox my passion = God's passion.

Coy, *v.t.* to fondle, caress. M.N.D. IV. I. 2. *v.i.* to disdain. Cor. V. I. 6.

Crack, *v.i.* to boast. *sb.* an urchin.

Crank, *sb.* winding passage. *v.i.* to wind, twist.

Crants, *sb.* garland, chaplet.

Crare, *sb.* a small sailing vessel.

Crisp, *adj.* curled.

Cross, *sb.* a coin (stamped with a cross).

Cross-row, *sb.* alphabet.

Crow-keeper, *sb.* a boy, or scare-crow, to keep crows from corn.

Cullion, *sb.* a base fellow.

Cunning, *sb.* knowledge, skill. *adj.* knowing, skilful, skilfully wrought.

Curb, *v.i.* to bow, cringe obsequiously.

Curdied, *p.p.* congealed.

Curiosity, *sb.* scrupulous nicety.

Curst, *adj.* bad-tempered.

Curtal, *adj.* having a docked tail. *sb.* a dock-tailed horse.

Customer, *sb.* a loose woman.

Cut, *sb.* a bobtailed horse.

Cuttle, *sb.* a bully.

Daff, *v.t.* to doff. Daff aside = thrust aside slightingly.

Darraign, *v.t.* to arrange, order the ranks for battle.

Dash, *sb.* mark of disgrace.

Daubery, *sb.* false pretence, cheat.

Day-woman, *sb.* dairy-woman.

Debosht, *p.p.* debauched.

Deck, *sb.* pack of cards.

Deem, *sb.* doom; opinion.

Defeat, *v.t.* to disguise. Oth. I. 3. 333. Destroy. Oth. IV. 2. 160.

Defeature, *sb.* disfigurement.

Defend, *v.t.* to forbid.

Defuse, *v.t.* to disorder and make unrecognizable.

Defused, *p.p.* disordered, shapeless.

Demerit, *sb.* desert.

Denier, *sb.* a small French coin.

Dern, *adj.* secret, dismal.

Detect, *v.t.* to discover, disclose.

Determinate, *p.p.* determined upon. Tw.N. II. 1. 10. Decided. Oth. IV. 2. 229. Ended. Sonn. LXXXVII. 4. *v.t.* bring to an end. R II. I. 3.

Dich, *v.i.* do to, happen to.

Diet, *v.t.* keep strictly, as if by a prescribed regimen.

Diffidence, *sb.* distrust, suspicion.

Digression, *sb.* transgression.

Diminutives, *sb.* the smallest of coins.

Directitude, *sb.* a blunder for some word unknown. Cor. IV. 5. 205.

Disanimate, *v.t.* to discourage.

Disappointed, *p.p.* unprepared.

Discandy, *v.i.* to thaw, melt.

Discipled, *p.p.* taught.

Disclose, *v.t.* to hatch. *sb.* the breaking of the shell by the chick on hatching.

Disme, *sb.* a tenth.

Distain, *v.t.* to stain, pollute.

Dive-dapper, *sb.* dabchick.

Dividant, *adj.* separate, different.

Dotant, *sb.* dotard.

Doubt, *sb.* fear, apprehension.

Dout, *v.t.* to extinguish.

Dowlas, *sb.* coarse linen.

Dowle, *sb.* down, the soft plumage of a feather.

Down-gyved, *adj.* hanging down about the ankle like gyves.

Dribbling, *adj.* weakly shot.

Drugs, *sb.* drudges.

Drumble, *v.i.* to be sluggish or clumsy.

Dry-beat, *v.t.* to cudgel, thrash.

Dry-foot. To draw dry-foot, track by scent.

Dudgeon, *sb.* the handle of a dagger.

Due, *v.t.* to endue.

Dump, *sb.* a sad strain.

Dup, *v.t.* to open.

Ean, *v.i.* to yean, lamb.

Ear, *v.t.* to plough, till.

Eche, *v.t.* to eke out.

Eftest, *adv.* readiest.

Eftsoons, *adv.* immediately.

Egal, *adj.* equal.

Egally, *adv.* equally.

Eisel, *sb.* vinegar.

Elf, *v.t.* to mat hair in a tangle; believed to be the work of elves.

Emballing, *sb.* investiture with the crown and sceptre.

Embarquement, *sb.* hindrance, restraint.

Ember-eyes, *sb.* vigils of Ember days.

Embowelled, *p.p.* emptied, exhausted.

Emmew, *v.t.* perhaps to mew up.

Empiricutic, *adj.* empirical, quackish.

Emulation, *sb.* jealous rivalry.

Enacture, *sb.* enactment, performance.

Encave, *v.t.* to hide, conceal.

Encumbered, *p.p.* folded.

End, *sb.* still an end = continually.

End, *v.t.* to get in the harvest.

Englut, *v.t.* to swallow.

Enlargement, *sb.* liberty, liberation.

Enormous, *adj.* out of the norm, monstrous.

Enseamed, *p.p.* defiled, filthy.

Ensear, *v.t.* to sear up, make dry.

Enshield, *adj.* enshielded, protected.

Entertain, *v.t.* to take into one's service.

Entertainment, *sb.* service.

Entreat, *v.t.* to treat.

Entreatments, *sb.* invitations.

Ephesian, *sb.* boon companion.

Eryngoes, *sb.* roots of the sea-holly, a supposed aphrodisiac.

Escot, *v.t.* to pay for.

Espial, *sb.* a spy.

Even Christian, *sb.* fellow Christian.

Excrement, *sb.* anything that grows out of the body, as hair, nails, etc. Used of the beard. M. of V. III. 2. 84. Of the hair. C. of E. II. 2. 79. Of the moustache. L.L.L. V. I. 98.

Exhibition, *sb.* allowance, pension.
Exigent, *sb.* end. 1 H VI. II. 5. 9. Exigency, critical need. J.
   C. V. 1. 19.
Exion, *sb.* blunder for action.
Expiate, *v.t* . to terminate. Sonn. XXII. 4.
Expiate, *p.p.* ended. R III. III. 3. 24.
Exsufflicate,   *adj.*   inflated,   both   literally   and
   metaphorically.
Extent, *sb.* seizure. As III. 1. 17. Violent attack. Tw.N. IV. 1.
   51. Condescension, favour. Ham. II. 2. 377. Display. T.
   A. IV. 4. 3.
Extraught, *p.p.* extracted.
Extravagancy, *sb.* vagrancy, aimless wandering about.
Eyas, *sb.* a nestling, a young hawk just taken from the nest.
Eyas-musket, *sb.* the young sparrow-hawk.
Eye, *v.i.* to appear, look to the eye.

Facinerious, *adj.* wicked.
Fadge, *v.i.* to succeed, suit.
Fading, *sb.* the burden of a song.
Fair, *v.t.* to make beautiful.
Fairing, *sb.* a gift.
Faitor, *sb.* evil-doer.
Fangled, *adj.* fond of novelties.
Fap, *adj.* drunk.
Farced, *p.p.* stuffed out.
Fardel, *sb.* a burden, bundle.
Fat, *adj.* cloying. *sb.* vat.
Favour, *sb.* outward appearance, aspect. In pl. = features.
Fear, *v.t.* to frighten. 3 H VI. III. 3. 226. Fear for. M. of V.
   III. 5. 3.
Feat, *adj.* neat, dexterous.
Feat, *v.t.* to fashion, form.
Fee, *sb.* worth, value.
Feeder, *sb.* servant.
Fee-farm, *sb.* a tenure without limit of time.
Fellowly, *adj.* companionable, sympathetic.

Feodary, *sb.* confederate.

Fere, *sb.* spouse, consort.

Ferret, *v.t.* to worry.

Festinate, *adj.* swift, speedy.

Fet, *p.p.* fetched.

Fico, *sb.* a fig (Span.).

File, *sb.* list.

File, *v.t.* to defile. Mac. III. 1. 65. Smooth, polish. L.L.L. V. I. II. *v.i.* to walk in file. H VIII. III. 2. 171.

Fill-horse, *sb.* a shaft-horse.

Fills, *sb.* shafts.

Fineless, *adj.* endless, infinite.

Firago, *sb.* virago.

Firk, *v.t.* to beat.

Fitchew, *sb.* pole-cat.

Fitment, *sb.* that which befits.

Flap-dragon, *sb.* snap-dragon, or small burning object, lighted and floated in a glass of liquor, to be swallowed burning. L.L.L. V. 1. 43. 2 H IV. II. 4. 244. *v.t.* to swallow like a flap-dragon. W.T. III. 3.100.

Flaw, *sb.* gust of wind. Ham. V. 1. 223. Small flake of ice. 2 H IV. IV. 4. 35. Passionate outburst. M. for M. II. 3. 11. A crack. Lear, II. 4. 288. *v.t.* make a flaw in, break. H VIII. I. 1. 95; I. 2. 21.

Fleer, *sb.* sneer. Oth. IV. 1. 83. *v.i.* to grin; sneer. L.L.L. V. 2. 109.

Fleshment, *sb.* encouragement given by first success.

Flewed, *p.p.* with large hanging chaps.

Flight, *sb.* a long light arrow.

Flighty, *adj.* swift.

Flirt-gill, *sb.* light wench.

Flote, *sb.* sea.

Flourish, *v.t.* to ornament, gloss over.

Fobbed, *p.p.* cheated, deceived.

Foil, *sb.* defeat. 1 H VI. III. 3. 11. *v.t.* to defeat, mar. Pass. P. 99

Foin, *v.i.* to thrust (in fencing).

Fopped, *p.p.* cheated, fooled.

Forbod, *p.p.* forbidden.

Fordo, *v.t.* to undo, destroy.

Foreign, *adj.* dwelling abroad.

Fork, *sb.* the forked tongue of a snake. M. for M. III. 1. 16. The barbed head of an arrow. Lear, I. 1. 146. The junction of the legs with the trunk. Lear. IV. 6. 120.

Forked, *p.p.* barbed. As II. 1. 24. Horned as a cuckold. T. & C. I. 2. 164.

Forslow, *v.i.* to delay.

Forspeak, *v.t.* to speak against.

Fosset-seller, *sb.* a seller of taps.

Fox, *sb.* broadsword.

Foxship, *sb.* selfish and ungrateful, cunning.

Fracted, *p.p.* broken.

Frampold, *adj.* turbulent, quarrelsome.

Frank, *v.t.* to pen in a frank or sty. R III. I. 3. 314. *sb.* a sty. 2 H IV. II. 2. 145. *adj.* liberal. Lear, III. 4. 20.

Franklin, *sb.* a yeoman.

Fraught, *sb.* freight, cargo, load. Tw.N. V. 1. 59. *v.t.* to load, burden. Cym. I. 1. 126. *p.p.* laden. M. of V. II. 8. 30. Stored. Two G. III. 2. 70.

Fraughtage, *sb.* cargo. C. of E. IV. 1. 8.

Fraughting, *part. adj.* constituting the cargo.

Frize, *sb.* a kind of coarse woollen cloth with a nap.

Frontier, *sb.* an outwork in fortification. 1 H IV. II. 3. 56. Used figuratively. 1 H IV. I. 3. 19.

Fruitful, *adj.* bountiful, plentiful.

Frush, *v.t.* to bruise, batter.

Frutify, blunder for certify. M. of V II. 2. 132.

Fubbed off, *p.p.* put off with excuses. 2 H IV. II. 1. 34.

Fullams, *sb.* a kind of false dice.

Gad, *sb.* a pointed instrument. T.A. IV. 1. 104. Upon the gad = on the spur of the moment, hastily. Lear, I. 2. 26.

Gage, *v.t.* to pledge.

Gaingiving, *sb.* misgiving.

Galliard, *sb.* a lively dance.

Gallimaufry, *sb.* medley, tumble.

Gallow, *v.t.* to frighten.

Gallowglass, *sb.* heavy-armed Irish foot-soldier.

Gallows, *sb.* a rogue, one fit to be hung.

Gallows-bird, *sb.* one that merits hanging.

Garboil, *sb.* uproar, commotion.

Gaskins, *sb.* loose breeches.

Gastness, *sb.* ghastliness, terror.

Geck, *sb.* dupe.

Generation, *sb.* offspring.

Generous, *adj.* nobly born.

Gennet, *sb.* a Spanish horse.

Gentry, *sb.* rank by birth. M.W.W. II. 1. 51. Courtesy. Ham. II. 2. 22.

German, *sb.* a near kinsman.

Germen, *sb.* germ, seed.

Gest, *sb.* a period of sojourn; originally the halting place in a royal progress.

Gib, *sb.* an old rom-cat.

Gibbet, *v.t.* to hang, as a barrel when it is slung.

Gig, *sb.* top.

Giglot, *adj.* wanton. 1 H VI. IV. 7. 41. *sb.* M. for M. V. 1. 345.

Gillyvors, *sb.* gillyflowers.

Gimmal-bit, *sb.* a double bit, or one made with double rings.

Gimmer, *sb.* contrivance, mechanical device.

Ging, *sb.* gang, pack.

Gird, *sb.* a scoff, jest. 2 H VI. III. 1. 131. *v.t.* to taunt, gibe at. 2 H IV. I. 2. 6.

Gleek, *sb.* scoff. 1 H VI. IV. 2. 12. *v.i.* to scoff. M.N.D. III. 1. 145.

Glib, *v.t.* to geld.

Gloze, *v.i.* to comment. H V. I. 2. 40. T. & C. II. 2. 165. To use flattery. R II. II. 1. 10; T.A. IV. 4. 35.

Gnarling, *pr.p.* snarling.

Godden, *sb.* good den, good even.

God'ild, God yield, God reward.

God-jer = good-year.

Good-year, *sb.* a meaningless interjection. M.A. I. 3. I.
  Some malific power. Lear, V. 3. 24.

Goss, *sb.* gorse.

Gossip, *sb.* sponsor. Two G. III. I. 269. *v.t.* to stand
  sponsor for. A. W. I. I. 176.

Gorbellied, *adj.* big-bellied.

Graff, *sb.* graft, scion. *v.t.* to graft.

Grain, *sb.* a fast colour. Hence in grain = ingrained.

Gratillity, *sb.* gratuity.

Gratulate, *adj.* gratifying.

Greek, *sb.* boon companion.

Grise, *sb.* a step.

Guard, *v.t.* to trim, ornament.

Guardant, *sb.* sentinel, guard.

Guidon, *sb.* standard, banner.

Gules, *adj.* red, in heraldry.

Gust, *sb.* taste. *v.t.* to taste.

Hackney, *sb.* loose woman.

Haggard, *sb.* untrained hawk.

Haggled, *p.p.* hacked, mangled.

Hair, *sb.* texture, nature. I H IV. IV. I. 61. Against the hair
  = against the grain. R. & J. II. 3. 97.

Handfast, *sb.* betrothal, contract. Cym. I. 5. 78. Custody.
  W.T. IV. 3. 778.

Handsaw, *sb.* corruption of heronshaw, a heron.

Hardiment, *sb.* daring deed.

Harlot, *adj.* lewd, base.

Hatched, *p.p.* closed with a hatch or half door. Per. IV. 2.
  33. Engraved. T. & C. I. 3. 65.

Havoc, to cry havoc = cry no quarter. John, II. I. 357. *v.t.*
  cut to pieces, destroy. H V. I. 2. 193.

Hawking, *adj.* hawk-like.

Hay, *sb.* a round dance. L.L.L. V. 1. 147. A term in fencing when a hit is made (Ital. *hai*, you have it). R. & J. II. 4. 27.

Hebenon, *sb.* perhaps the yew (Germ. *Eiben*). Ebony and henbane have been suggested.

Hefts, *sb.* heavings.

Helm, *v.t.* to steer.

Helpless, *adj.* not helping, useless. R III. I. 2. 13; Lucr. 1027. Incurable, Lucr. 756.

Hent, *sb.* grasp, hold. Ham. III. 3. 88. *v.t.* to hold, pass. M. for M. IV. 6. 14.

Hermit, *sb.* beadsman, one bound to pray for another.

Hild = held.

Hilding, *sb.* a good-for-nothing.

Hoar, *adj.* mouldy, R. & J. II. 3. 136. *v.i.* to become mouldy. R. & J. II. 3. 142.

Hoar, *v.t.* to make hoary or white, as with leprosy.

Hobby-horse, *sb.* a principal figure in the old morris dance. L.L.L. III. 1. 30. A light woman. M.A. III. 2. 68.

Hob-nob, have or not have, hit or miss.

Hold in, *v.i.* to keep counsel.

Holding, *sb.* the burden of a song. A. & C. II. 7. 112. Fitness, sense. A.W. IV. 2. 27.

Holy-ales, *sb.* rural festivals.

Honest, *adj.* chaste.

Honesty, *sb.* chastity. M.W.W. II. 2. 234. Decency. Tw.N. II. 3. 85. Generosity, liberality. Tim. III. 1. 30.

Honey-seed, blunder for homicide, 2 H IV. II. 1. 52.

Honey-suckle, blunder for homicidal. 2 H IV. II. 1. 50.

Hoodman, *sb.* the person blinded in the game of hoodman-blind.

Hoodman-blind, *sb.* blind-man's buff.

Hot at hand, not to be held in.

Hot-house, *sb.* bagnio, often in fact a brothel as well.

Hox, *v.t.* to hough, hamstring.

Hoy, *sb.* a small coasting vessel.

Hugger-mugger, In, stealthily and secretly.

Hull, *v.i.* to float.

Hulling, *pr. p.* floating at the mercy of the waves.

Ignomy, *sb.* ignominy.
Imbar, *v.t.* to bar in, make secure. H V. I. 2. 94.
Imboss, *v.t.* to hunt to death.
Imbossed, *p.p.* swollen. As II. 7. 67. Foaming at the mouth.
    T. of S. Ind. I. 16.
Immanity, *sb.* savageness, ferocity.
Immoment, *adj.* insignificant.
Immures, *sb.* surrounding walls.
Imp, *v.t.* to graft new feathers to a falcon's wing.
Impair, *adj.* unsuitable.
Impale, *v.t.* to encircle.
Impart, *v.t.* to afford, grant. Lucr. 1039; Sonn. LXXII. 8.
    v.i. to behave oneself. Ham. I. 2. 112.
Imperceiverant, *adj.* lacking in perception.
Impeticos, *v.t.* to put in the petticoat or pocket.
Importance, *sb.* importunity. John, II. 1. 7. Import. W.T.
    V. 2. 19. Question at issue, that which is imported.
    Cym. I. 5. 40.
Imposition, *sb.* command, injunction. M. of V. I. 2. 106.
    Penalty. M. for M. I. 2. 186.
Imposthume, *sb.* abscess.
Imprese, *sb.* device with a motto.
Include, *v.t.* to conclude, end.
Incontinent, *adj.* immediate.
Incony, *adj.* dainty, delicate.
Indent, *v.i.* to make terms.
Index, *sb.* introduction (in old books the index came first).
Indifferency, *sb.* impartiality.
Indirectly, *adv.* wrongly, unjustly.
Indurance, *sb.* durance, imprisonment.
Infest, *v.t.* to vex, trouble.
Inherit, *v.t.* to possess. Tp. IV. I. 154. To cause to possess,
    put in possession. R II. I. I. 85. *v.i.* to take possession.
    Tp. II. 2. 182.
Inheritor, *sb.* possessor.

Injury, *sb*. insult.

Inkhorn mate, *sb*. bookworm.

Inkle, *sb*. coarse tape.

Insisture, *sb*. persistence.

Intenible, *adj*. incapable of holding.

Intention, *sb*. aim, direction.

Intermissive, *adj*. intermitted, interrupted.

Intrinse, *adj*. tightly drawn.

Invised, *adj*. unseen, a doubtful word.

Irregulous, *adj*. lawless.

Jack, *sb*. figure that struck the bell in old clocks. R III. IV. 2. 114. A term of contempt. R III. I. 3. 72. The small bowl aimed at in the game of bowls. Cym. II. I. 2. The key of a virginal. Sonn. CXXVIII. 5. A drinking vessel. T. of S. IV. 1. 48.

Jade, *v.t.* to play the jade with, run away with. Tw.N. II. 5. 164. Drive like a jade. A. & C. III. 1. 34. Treat with contempt. H VIII. III. 2. 280.

Jakes, *sb*. a privy.

Jar, *sb*. a tick of the clock. W.T. I. 2. 43.

Jar, *v.t.* to tick. R II. V. 5. 51. *v.i.* to guard. 1 H VI. III. 1. 70. *sb*. a quarrel. 1 H VI. I. 1. 44.

Jesses, *sb*. straps attaching the legs of a hawk to the fist.

Jet, *v.i.* to strut. Tw.N. II. 4. 32. Advance threateningly. R III. II. 4. 51.

Journal, *adj*. diurnal, daily.

Jowl, *v.t.* to knock, dash.

Kam, *adj*. crooked, away from the point.

Keech, *sb*. a lump of tallow or fat.

Keel, *v.t.* to cool.

Ken, *sb*. perception, sight. *v.t.* to know.

Kern, *sb*. light-armed foot-soldier of Ireland.

Kibe, *sb*. chilblain on the heel.

Kicky-wicky, *sb*. a pet name.

Killen = to kill.

Kiln-hole, *sb*. the fireplace of an oven or kiln.

Kind, *sb.* nature. M. of V. I. 3. 84. *adj.* natural. Lucr. 1423. *adv.* kindly. Tim. I. 2. 224.

Kindle, *v.t.* to bring forth young. As III. 2. 343. Incite. As I. 1. 179.

Knack, *sb.* a pretty trifle.

Knap, *v.t.* to gnaw, nibble. M. of V. III. 1. 9. Rap. Lear, II. 4. 123.

Laboursome, *adj.* elaborate.

Laced mutton, *sb.* slang for courtesan.

Lade, *v.t.* to empty, drain.

Land-damn. Unrecognizably corrupt word in W.T. II. 1. 143.

Lapsed, *p.p.* caught, surprised. Tw.N. III. 3. 36.

Latch, *v.t.* to catch, lay hold of.

Latten, *sb.* a mixture of copper and tin. M.W.W. I. 1. 153.

Laund, *sb.* glade.

Lavolt, *sb.* a dance in which two persons bound high and whirl round.

Lay for, *v.t.* to strive to win.

Leasing, *sb.* lying, falsehood.

Leave, *sb.* liberty, license.

Leer, *sb.* complexion.

Leese, *v.t.* to lose.

Leet, *sb.* a manor court. T. of S. Ind. II. 87. The time when such is held. Oth. III. 3. 140.

Leiger, *sb.* ambassador.

Length, *sb.* delay.

Let, *v.t.* to hinder. Tw.N. V. 1. 246; Ham. I. 4. 85. Detain. W.T. I. 2. 41. Forbear. Lucr. 10. *p.p.* caused. Ham. IV. 6. 11. *sb.* hindrance. H V. V. 2. 65.

Let-alone, *sb.* hindrance, prohibition.

Level, *sb.* aim, line of fire. R. & J. III. 3. 102. *v.i.* to aim. R III. IV. 4. 202. Be on the same level. Oth. I. 3. 239. *adv.* evenly. Tw.N. II. 4. 32.

Lewd, *adj.* base, vile.

Libbard, *sb.* leopard.

Liberal, *adj.* licentious. Liberal conceit = elaborate design. Ham. V. 2. 152. *adv.* freely, openly. Oth. V. 2. 220.

Lieger, *sb.* ambassador.

Lifter, *sb.* thief.

Light, *p.p.* lighted.

Likelihood, *sb.* sign, indication.

Lime, *v.t.* to put lime into liquor. M.W.W. I. 3. 14. Smear with bird-lime. 2 H VI. I. 3. 86. Catch with bird-lime. Tw.N. III. 4. 75. Cement. 3 H VI. V. 1. 84.

Limit, *sb.* appointed time. R II. I. 3. 151. *v.t.* to appoint. John. V. 2. 123.

Line, *v.t.* to draw, paint. As III. 2. 93. Strengthen, fortify. 1 H IV. II. 3. 85.

Line-grove, *sb.* a grove of lime trees.

Linsey-woolsey, *sb.* gibberish (literally, mixed stuff).

Lipsbury pinfold. Perhaps = between the teeth.

List, *sb.* desire, inclination. Oth. II. 1. 105. Limit, boundary. 1 H IV. IV. 1. 51. Lists for combat. Mac. III. 1. 70.

Lither, *adj.* flexible, gentle.

Livery, *sb.* delivery of a freehold into the possession of the heir.

Lob, *sb.* lubber, lout.

Lockram, *sb.* coarse linen.

Lodge, *v.t.* to lay flat, beat down.

Loggats, *sb.* a game somewhat resembling bowls.

Loof, *v.t.* to luff, bring close to the wind.

Losel, *sb.* a wasteful, worthless fellow.

Lout, *v.t.* to make a lout or fool of.

Lown, *sb.* base fellow.

Luce, *sb.* pike or jack.

Lurch, *v.t.* to win a love set at a game; bear off the prize easily. Cor. II. 2. 102. *v.i.* to skulk. M. W. W. II. 2. 25.

Lym, *sb.* bloodhound; so called from the leam or leash used to hold him.

Maggot-pie, *sb.* magpie.

Main, *sb.* a call at dice. 1 H IV. IV. 1. 47. Mainland. Lear, III. 1. 6. The chief power. Ham. V. 4. 15.

Main-course, *sb.* mainsail.

Main'd, *p.p.* maimed.

Makeless, *adj.* mateless, widowed.

Malkin, *sb.* slattern.

Mallard, *sb.* a wild drake.

Mallecho, *sb.* mischief (Span. *malhecho*).

Malt-horse, *sb.* brewer's horse.

Mammering, *pr.p.* hesitating.

Mammet, *sb.* a doll.

Mammock, *v.t.* to tear in pieces.

Manakin, *sb.* little man.

Mankind, *adj.* masculine, applied to a woman.

Manner, with the = in the act, red-handed.

Mare, *sb.* nightmare. To ride the wild mare = play at see-saw.

Mark, *sb.* thirteen shillings and fourpence.

Mart, *v.i.* to market, traffic. Cym. I. 6. 150. *v.t.* to vend, traffic with. J. C. IV. 3. 11.

Mastic, *sb.* used to stop decayed teeth.

Match, *sb.* compact, bargain. M. of V. III. 1. 40. Set a match = make an appointment. 1 H IV. 1. 2. 110.

Mate, *v.t.* to confound, make bewildered. C. of E. III. 2. 54. Match, cope with. H VIII. III. 2. 274.

Material, *adj.* full of matter.

Maugre, *prep.* in spite of.

Maund, *sb.* a basket.

Mazard, *sb.* skull.

Meacock, *adj.* spiritless, pusillanimous.

Mealed. *p.p.* mingled, compounded.

Mean, *sb.* the intermediate part between the tenor and treble.

Meiny, *sb.* attendants, retinue.

Mell, *v.i.* to meddle.

Mered, He being the mered question—the question concerning him alone. A. & C. III. 13. 10.

Mess, *sb,* a set of four. L.L.L. IV. 3. 204. Small quantity. 2 H IV. II. 1. 95. Lower messes = inferiors, as messing at the lower end of the table. W.T. I. 2. 226.

Mete, *v. i.* to mete at = aim at.

Metheglin, *sb.* a kind of mead, made of honey and water.

Micher, *sb.* truant.

Miching, *adj.* sneaking, stealthy.

Mineral, *sb.* a mine.

Minikin, *adj.* small, pretty.

Minion, *sb.* darling, favourite. John, II. 1. 392. Used contemptuously. 2 H VI. I. 3. 82. A pert, saucy person. 2 H VI. I. 3. 136.

Mirable, *adj.* admirable.

Mire, *v.i.* to be bemired, sink as into mire.

Misdread, *sb.* fear of evil.

Misprision, *sb.* mistake. M.N.D. III. 2. 90. Contempt. A.W. II. 3. 153.

Misproud, *adj.* viciously proud.

Miss, *sb.* misdoing.

Missingly, *adv.* regretfully.

Missive, *sb.* messenger.

Misthink, *v.t.* to misjudge.

Mobled, *p.p.* having the face or head muffled.

Modern, *adj.* commonplace, trite.

Module, *sb.* mould, form.

Moldwarp, *sb.* mole.

Mome, *sb.* blockhead, dolt.

Momentany, *adj.* momentary, lasting an instant.

Monster, *v.t.* to make monstrous.

Month's mind, *sb.* intense desire or yearning.

Moralize, *v.t.* to interpret, explain.

Mort, *sb.* trumpet notes blown at the death of the deer.

Mortal, *adj.* deadly.

Mortified, *p.p.* deadened, insensible.

Mot, *sb.* motto, device.

Mother, *sb.* the disease *hysterica passio.*

Motion, *v.t.* to propose, counsel. 1 H VI. I. 3. 63. *sb.* a puppet show. W.T. IV. 3. 96. A puppet. Two G. II. 1. 91. Solicitation, proposal, suit. C. of E. I. 1. 60. Emotion, feeling, impulse. Tw.N. II. 4. 18.

Motive, *sb.* a mover, instrument, member.

Mountant, *adj.* lifted up.

Mow, *sb.* a grimace. *v.i.* to grimace.

Moy, *sb.* probably some coin.

Muleter, *sb. muleteer.*

Mulled, *p.p.* flat, insipid.

Mummy, *sb.* a medical or magical preparation originally
    made from mummies.

Murdering-piece, *sb.* a cannon loaded with chain-shot.

Murrion, *adj.* infected with the murrain.

Muse, *v.i.* to wonder. John, III. 1. 317. *v.t.* to wonder at.
    Tp. III. 3. 36.

Muset, *sb.* a gap or opening in a hedge.

Muss, *sb.* scramble.

Mutine, *sb.* mutineer.

Mystery, *sb.* profession. M. for M. IV. 2. 28. Professional
    skill. A.W. III. 6. 65.

Nayword, *sb.* pass-word, M.W.W. II. 2. 126. A by-word.
    Tw.N. II. 3. 132.

Neat, *adj.* trim, spruce.

Neb, *sb.* bill or beak.

Neeld, *sb.* needle.

Neeze, *v.i.* to sneeze.

Neif, *sb.* fist.

Next, *adj.* nearest.

Nick, *sb.* out of all nick, beyond all reckoning.

Night-rule, *sb.* revelry.

Nill = will not.

Nine-men's-morris, *sb.* a rustic game.

Note, *sb.* list, catalogue. W.T. IV. 2. 47. Note of
    expectation = list of expected guests. Mac. III. 3. 10.
    Stigma, mark of reproach. R II. 1. 1. 43. Distinction.
    Cym. II. 3. 12. knowledge, observation. Lear, III. 1. 18.

Nott-pated, *adj.* crop-headed.

Nousle, *v.t.* to nurse, nourish delicately.

Nowl, *sb.* noddle.

Nuthook, *sb.* slang for catchpole.

Oathable, *adj.* capable of taking an oath.

Object, *sb.* anything presented to the sight; everything that comes in the way.

Obsequious, *adj.* regardful of funeral rites. 3 H VI. II. 5. 118. Funereal, having to do with obsequies. T. A. V. 3. 153.

Observance, *sb.* observation. Oth. III. 3. 151. Homage. 2 H IV. IV. 3. 15. Ceremony. M. of V. II. 2. 194.

Obstacle, *sb.* blunder for obstinate.

Occupation, *sb.* trade (in contemptuous sense). Cor. IV. 1. 14. Voice of occupation = vote of working men. Cor. IV. 6. 98.

Odd, *adj.* unnoticed. Tp. I. 2. 223. At odds. T. & C. IV. 5. 265.

Oeillades, *sb.* amorous glances.

O' ergrown, *p.p.* bearded. Cym. IV. 4. 33. Become too old. M. for M. I. 3. 22.

O'erstrawed, *p.p.* overstrewn.

Office, *v.t.* to office all = do all the domestic service. A. W. III. 2. 128. Keep officiously. Cor. V. 2. 61.

Oneyers, *sb.* unexplained word.

Opposition, *sb.* combat, encounter.

Orb, *sb.* orbit. R. & J. II. 1. 151. Circle. M.N.D. II. 1. 9. A heavenly body. M. of V. V. 1. 60. The earth. Tw.N. III. 1. 39.

Ordinant, *adj.* ordaining, controlling.

Ordinary, *sb.* a public dinner at which each man pays for his own share.

Ort, *sb.* remnant, refuse.

Ouphs, *sb.* elves, goblins.

Outrage, *sb.* outburst of rage.

Overscutch'd, *p.p.* over-whipped, over-switched (perhaps in a wanton sense).

Overture, *sb.* disclosure. W.T. II. 1. 172. Declaration. Tw.N. I. 5. 208.

Owe, *v.t.* to own, possess.

Packing, *sb.* plotting, conspiracy.

Paddock, *sb.* toad. Ham. III. 4. 191. A familiar spirit in the form of a toad. Mac. I. 1. 9.

Pajock, *sb.* term of contempt, by some said to mean peacock.

Pale, *sb.* enclosure, confine.

Palliament, *sb.* robe.

Parcel-bawd, *sb.* half-bawd.

Paritor, *sb.* apparitor, an officer of the Bishops' Court.

Part, *sb.* party, side.

Partake, *v.t.* to make to partake, impart. W.T. V. 3. 132. To share. J.C. II. 1. 305.

Parted, *p.p.* endowed.

Partisan, *sb.* a kind of pike.

Pash, *sb.* a grotesque word for the head. W.T. I. 2. 128. *v.t.* to smite, dash. T. & C. II. 3. 202.

Pass, *v.t.* to pass sentence on. M. for M. II. 1. 19. Care for. 2 H VI. IV. 2. 127. Represent. L.L.L. V. 1. 123. Make a thrust in fencing. Tw.N. III. 1. 44.

Passage, *sb.* passing to and fro. C. of E. III. 1. 99. Departure, death. Ham. III. 3. 86. Passing away. 1 H VI. II. 5. 108. Occurrence. A.W. I. 1. 19. Process, course. R. & J. Prol. 9. Thy passages of life = the actions of thy life. 1 H IV. III. 2. 8. Passages of grossness = gross impositions. Tw.N. III. 2. 70. Motion. Cor. V. 6. 76.

Passant. In heraldry, the position of an animal walking.

Passion, *sb.* passionate poem. M.N.D. V. 1. 306; Sonn. XX. 2.

Passionate, *v.t.* to express with emotion. T.A. III. 2. 6. *adj.* displaying emotion. 2 H VI. I. 1. 104. Sorrowful. John, II. 1. 544.

Passy measures, a corruption of the Italian *passamezzo*, denoting a stately and measured step in dancing.

Patch, *sb.* fool.

Patchery, *sb.* knavery, trickery.

Patronage, *v.t.* to patronize, protect.

Pavin, *sb.* a stately dance of Spanish or Italian origin.

Pawn, *sb.* a pledge.

Peach, *v.t.* to impeach, accuse.

Peat, *sb.* pet, darling.

Pedascule, *sb.* vocative, pedant, schoolmaster.

Peevish, *adj.* childish, silly. 1 H VI. V. 3. 186. Fretful, wayward. M. of V. I. 1. 86.

Peise, *v.t.* to poise, balance. John, II. 1. 575. Retard by making heavy. M. of V. III. 2. 22. Weigh down. R III. V. 3. 106.

Pelt, *v.i.* to let fly with words of opprobrium.

Pelting, *adj.* paltry.

Penitent, *adj.* doing penance.

Periapt, *sb.* amulet.

Period, *sb.* end, conclusion. A. & C. IV. 2. 25. *v.t.* to put an end to. Tim. I. 1. 103.

Perked up, *p.p.* dressed up.

Perspective, *sb.* glasses so fashioned as to create an optical illusion.

Pert, *adj.* lively, brisk.

Pertaunt-like, *adv.* word unexplained and not yet satisfactorily amended. L.L.L. V. 2. 67.

Pervert, *v.t.* to avert, turn aside.

Pettitoes, *sb.* feet; properly pig's feet.

Pheeze, *v.t.* beat, chastise, torment.

Phisnomy, *sb.* physiognomy.

Phraseless, *adj.* indescribable.

Physical, *adj.* salutary, wholesome.

Pia mater, *sb.* membrane that covers the brain; used for the brain itself.

Pick, *v.t.* to pitch, throw.

Picked, *p.p.* refined, precise.

Picking, *adj.* trifling, small.

Piece, *sb.* a vessel of wine.

Pight, *p.p.* pitched.

Piled, *p.p* = peeled, bald, with quibble on 'piled' of velvet.

Pill, *v.t.* to pillage, plunder.

Pin, *sb.* bull's-eye of a target.

Pin-buttock, *sb.* a narrow buttock.

Pioned, *adj.* doubtful word: perhaps covered with marsh-marigold, or simply dug.

Pip, *sb.* a spot on cards. A pip out = intoxicated, with reference to a game called one and thirty.

Pitch, *sb.* the height to which a falcon soars, height.

Placket, *sb.* opening in a petticoat, or a petticoat.

Planched, *adj.* made of planks.

Plantage, *sb.* plants, vegetation.

Plantation, *sb.* colonizing.

Plausive, *adj.* persuasive, pleasing.

Pleached, *adj.* interlaced, folded.

Plurisy, *sb.* superabundance.

Point-devise, *adj.* precise, finical. L.L.L. V. 1.19. *adv.* Tw.N. II. 5. 162.

Poking-sticks, *sb.* irons for setting out ruffs.

Pole-clipt, *adj.* used of vineyards in which the vines are grown around poles.

Polled, *adj.* clipped, laid bare.

Pomander, *sb.* a ball of perfume.

Poor-John, *sb.* salted and dried hake.

Porpentine, *sb.* porcupine.

Portable, *adj.* supportable, endurable.

Portage, *sb.* port-hole. H V. III. 1. 10. Port-dues. Per. III. 1. 35.

Portance, *sb.* deportment, bearing.

Posse, *v.t.* to curdle.

Posy, *sb.* a motto on a ring.

Potch, *v.i.* to poke, thrust.

Pottle, *sb.* a tankard; strictly a two quart measure.

Pouncet-box, *sb.* a box for perfumes, pierced with holes.

Practice, *sb.* plot.

Practisant, *sb.* accomplice.

Practise, *v.i.* to plot, use stratagems. Two G. IV. 1. 47. *v.t.* to plot. John, IV. 1. 20.

Precedent, *sb.* rough draft. R III. III. 6. 7. Prognostic, indication. V. & A. 26.

Prefer, *v.t.* to promote, advance. Two G. II. 4. 154. Recommend. Cym. II. 3. 50. Present offer. M.N.D. IV. 2. 37.

Pregnant, *adj.* ready-witted, clever. Tw.N. II. 2. 28. Full of meaning. Ham. II. 2. 209. Ready. Ham. III. 2. 66. Plain, evident. M. for M. II. 1. 23.

Prenzie, *adj.* demure.

Pretence, *sb.* project, scheme.

Prick, *sb.* point on a dial. 3 H VI. I. 4. 34. Bull's-eye. L.L.L. IV. 1. 132. Prickle. As III. 2. 113. Skewer. Lear, II. 3. 16.

Pricket, *sb.* a buck of the second year.

Prick-song, *sb.* music sung from notes.

Prig, *sb.* a thief.

Private, *sb.* privacy. Tw.N. III. 4. 90. Private communication. John, IV. 3. 16.

Prize, *sb.* prize-contest. T.A. I. 1. 399. Privilege. 3 H VI. I. 4. 59. Value. Cym. III. 6. 76.

Probal, *adj.* probable, reasonable.

Proditor, *sb.* traitor.

Proface, *int.* much good may it do you!

Propagate, *v.t.* to augment.

Propagation, *sb.* augmentation.

Proper-false, *adj.* handsome and deceitful.

Property, *sb.* a tool or instrument. M.W.W. III. 4. 10. *v.t.* to make a tool of. John, V. 2. 79.

Pugging, *adj.* thievish.

Puisny, *adj.* unskilful, like a tyro.

Pun, *v.t.* to pound.

Punk, *sb.* strumpet.

Purchase, *v.t.* to acquire, get. *sb.* acquisition, booty.

Pursuivant, *sb.* a herald's attendant or messenger.

Pursy, *adj.* short-winded, asthmatic.

Puttock, *sb.* a kite.

Puzzel, *sb.* a filthy drab (Italian *puzzolente*).

Quaintly, *adv.* ingeniously, deliberately.

Qualification, *sb.* appeasement.

Quality, *sb.* profession, calling, especially that of an actor. Two G. IV. I. 58. Professional skill. Tp. I. 2. 193.

Quarter, *sb.* station. John, V. 5. 20. Keep fair quarter = keep on good terms with, be true to. C. of E. II. I. 108. In quarter = on good terms. Oth. II. 3. 176.

Quat, *sb.* pimple.

Quatch-buttock, *sb.* a squat or flat buttock.

Quean, *sb.* wench, hussy.

Queasiness, *sb.* nausea, disgust.

Queasy, *adj.* squeamish, fastidious. M.A. II. I. 368. Disgusted. A. & C. III. 6. 20.

Quell, *sb.* murder.

Quest, *sb.* inquest, jury. R III. I. 4. 177. Search, inquiry, pursuit. M. of V. I. I. 172. A body of searchers. Oth. I. 2. 46.

Questant, *sb.* aspirant, candidate.

Quicken, *v.t.* to make alive. A.W. II. I. 76. Refresh, revive. M. of V. II. 7. 52. *v.i.* to become alive, revive. Lear, III. 7. 40.

Quietus, *sb.* settlement of an account.

Quill, *sb.* body. 2 H VI. I. 3. 3.

Quillet, *sb.* quibble.

Quintain, *sb.* a figure set up for tilting at.

Quire, *sb.* company.

Quittance, *v.i.* to requite. 1 H VI. II. I. 14. *sb.* acquittance. M. W. W. I. I. 10. Requital. 2 H IV. I. I. 108.

Quoif, *sb.* cap.

Quoit, *v.t.* to throw.

Quote, *v.t.* to note, examine.

Rabato, *sb.* a kind of ruff.

Rabbit-sucker, *sb.* sucking rabbit.

Race, *sb.* root. W.T. IV. 3. 48. Nature, disposition. M. for M. II. 4. 160. Breed. Mac. II. 4. 15.

Rack, *v.t.* stretch, strain. M. of V. I. I. 181. Strain to the utmost. *Cor.* V. I. 16.

Rack, *sb.* a cloud or mass of clouds. Ham. II. 2. 492. *v.i.* move like vapour. 3 H VI. II. I. 27.

Rampired, *p.p.* fortified by a rampart.

Ramps, *sb.* wanton wenches.

Ranges, *sb.* ranks.

Rap, *v.t.* to transport.

Rascal, *sb.* a deer out of condition.

Raught, *impf.* & *p.p.* reached.

Rayed, *p.p.* befouled. T. of S. IV. 1. 3. In T. of S. III. 2. 52 it perhaps means arrayed, *i.e.* attacked.

Raze, *sb.* root.

Razed, *p.p.* slashed.

Reave, *v.t.* to bereave.

Rebate, *v.t.* to make dull, blunt.

Recheat, *sb.* a set of notes sounded to call hounds off a false scent.

Rede, *sb.* counsel.

Reechy, *adj.* smoky, grimy.

Refell, *v.t.* to refute.

Refuse, *sb.* rejection, disowning. *v.t.* to reject, disown.

Reguerdon, *v.t.* to reward, guerdon.

Remonstrance, *sb.* demonstration.

Remotion, *sb.* removal.

Renege, *v.t.* to deny.

Renying, *pres. p.* denying.

Replication, *sb.* echo. J.C. I. 1. 50. Reply. Ham. IV. 2. 12.

Rere-mice, *sb.* bats.

Respected, blunder for suspected.

Respective, *adj.* worthy of regard. Two G. IV. 4. 197. Showing regard. John, I. 1. 188. Careful. M. of V. V. 1. 156.

Respectively, *adv.* respectfully.

Rest, *sb.* set up one's rest is to stand upon the cards in one's hand, be fully resolved.

Resty, *adj.* idle, lazy.

Resume, *v.t.* to take.

Reverb, *v.t.* to resound.

Revolt, *sb.* rebel.

Ribaudred, *adj.* ribald, lewd.

Rid, *v.t.* to destroy, do away with.

Riggish, *adj.* wanton.

Rigol, *sb.* a circle.

Rim, *sb.* midriff or abdomen.

Rivage, *sb.* shore.

Rival, *sb.* partner, companion. M.N.D. III. 2. 156. *v.i.* to be a competitor. Lear, I. I. 191.

Rivality, *sb.* partnership, participation.

Rivelled, *adj.* wrinkled.

Road, *sb.* roadstead, port. Two G. II. 4. 185. Journey. H VIII. IV. 2. 17. Inroad, incursion. H V. I. 2. 138.

Roisting, *adj.* roistering, blustering.

Romage, *sb.* bustle, turmoil.

Ronyon, *sb.* scurvy wretch.

Rook, *v.i.* to cower, squat.

Ropery, *sb.* roguery.

Rope-tricks, *sb.* knavish tricks.

Roping, *pr.p.* dripping.

Roted, *p.p.* learned by heart.

Rother, *sb.* an ox, or animal of the ox kind.

Round, *v.i.* to whisper. John, II. I. 566. *v.t.* to surround. M.N.D. IV. I. 52.

Round, *adj.* straightforward, blunt, plainspoken. C. of E. II. I. 82.

Rouse, *sb.* deep draught, bumper.

Rout, *sb.* crowd, mob. C. of E. III. I. 101. Brawl. Oth. II. 3. 210.

Row, *sb.* verse or stanza.

Roynish, *adj.* scurvy; hence coarse, rough.

Rub, *v.i.* to encounter obstacles. L.L.L. IV. I. 139. Rub on, of a bowl that surmounts the obstacle in its course. T. & C. III. 2. 49. *sb.* impediment, hindrance; from the game of bowls. John, III. 4. 128.

Ruffle, *v.i.* to swagger, bully. T.A. I. I. 314.

Ruddock, *sb.* the redbreast.

Rudesby, *sb.* a rude fellow.

Rump-fed, *adj.* pampered; perhaps fed on offal, or else fat-rumped.

Running banquet, a hasty refreshment (fig.).

Rush aside, *v.t.* to pass hastily by, thrust aside.

Rushling, blunder for rustling.

Sad, *adj.* grave, serious. M. of V. II. 2. 195. Gloomy, sullen. R II. V. 5. 70.

Sagittary, *sb.* a centaur. T. & C. V. 5. 14. The official residence in the arsenal at Venice. Oth. I. 1. 160.

Sallet, *sb.* a close-fitting helmet. 2 H VI. IV. 10. 11. A salad. 2 H VI. IV. 10. 8.

Salt, *sb.* salt-cellar. Two G. III. 1. 354. *adj.* lecherous. M. for M. V. 1. 399. Stinging, bitter. T. & C. I. 3. 371.

Salutation, *sb.* give salutation to my blood = make my blood rise.

Salute, *v.t.* to meet. John, II. 1. 590. To affect. H VIII. II. 3. 103.

Sanded, *adj.* sandy-coloured.

Say, *sb.* a kind of silk.

Scald, *adj.* scurvy, scabby. H V. V. 1. 5.

Scale, *v.t.* to put in the scales, weigh.

Scall = scald. M.W.W. III. 1. 115.

Scamble, *v.i.* to scramble.

Scamel, *sb.* perhaps a misprint for seamell, or seamew.

Scantling, *sb.* a scanted or small portion.

Scape, *sb.* freak, escapade.

Sconce, *sb.* a round fort. H V. III. 6. 73. Hence a protection for the head. C. of E. II. 2. 37. Hence the skull. Ham. V. 1. 106. *v.r.* to ensconce, hide. Ham. III. 4. 4.

Scotch, *sb.* notch. *v.t.* to cut, slash.

Scrowl, *v.i.* perhaps for to scrawl.

Scroyles, *sb.* scabs, scrofulous wretches.

Scrubbed, *adj.* undersized.

Scull, *sb.* shoal of fish.

Seal, *sb.* to give seals = confirm, carry out.

Seam, *sb.* grease, lard.

Seconds, *sb.* an inferior kind of flour.

Secure, *adj.* without care, confident.

Security, *sb.* carelessness, want of caution.

Seedness, *sb.* sowing with seed.

Seel, *v.t.* to close up a hawk's eyes.

Self-admission, *sb.* self-approbation.

Semblative, *adj.* resembling, like.

Sequestration, *sb.* separation.

Serpigo, *sb.* tetter or eruption on the skin.

Sessa, *int.* exclamation urging to speed.

Shard-borne, *adj.* borne through the air on shards.

Shards, *sb.* the wing cases of beetles. A. & C. III. 2. 20.
   Potsherds. Ham. V. I. 254.

Sharked up, *p.p.* gathered indiscriminately.

Shealed, *p.p.* shelled.

Sheep-biter, *sb.* a malicious, niggardly fellow.

Shent, *p.p.* scolded, rebuked. M.W.W. I. 4. 36.

Shive, *sb.* slice.

Shog, *v.i.* to move, jog.

Shore, *sb.* a sewer.

Shrewd, *adj.* mischievous, bad.

Shrewdly, *adv.* badly.

Shrewdness, *sb.* mischievousness.

Shrieve, *sb.* sheriff.

Shrowd, *sb.* shelter, protection.

Siege, *sb.* seat. M. for M. IV. 2. 98. Rank. Ham. IV. 7. 75.
   Excrement. Tp. II. 2. III.

Significant, *sb.* sign, token.

Silly, *adj.* harmless, innocent. Two G. IV. I. 72. Plain,
   simple. Tw.N. II. 4. 46.

Simular, *adj.* simulated, counterfeited. Cym. V. 5. 20. *sb.*
   simulator, pretender. Lear, III. 2. 54.

Sitch, *adv.* and *conj.* since.

Skains-mates, *sb.* knavish companions.

Slab, *adj.* slabby, slimy.

Sleeve-hand, *sb.* wristband.

Sleided, *adj.* untwisted.

Slipper, *adj.* slippery.

Slobbery, *adj.* dirty.

Slubber, *v.t.* to slur over, do carelessly.

Smatch, *sb.* smack, taste.

Sneak-cup, *sb.* a fellow who shirks his liquor.

Sneap, *v.t.* to pinch, nip. L.L.L. I. I. 100. *sb.* snub, reprimand. 2 H IV. II. 1. 125.

Sneck up, contemptuous expression = go and be hanged.

Snuff, *sb.* quarrel. Lear, III. 1. 26. Smouldering wick of a candle. Cym. I. 6. 87. Object of contempt. A.W. I. 2. 60. Take in snuff = take offence at. L.L.L. V. 2. 22.

Sob, *sb.* a rest given to a horse to regain its wind.

Solidare, *sb.* a small coin.

Sonties, *sb.* corruption of saints.

Sooth, *sb.* flattery.

Soothers, *sb.* flatterers.

Sophy, *sb.* the Shah of Persia.

Sore, *sb.* a buck of the fourth year.

Sorel, *sb.* a buck of the third year.

Sort, *sb.* rank. M.A. I. 1. 6. Set, company. R III. V. 3. 316. Manner. M. of V. I. 2. 105. Lot. T. & C. I. 3. 376.

Sort, *v.t.* to pick out. Two G. III. 2. 92. To rank. Ham. II. 2. 270. To arrange, dispose. R III. II. 2. 148. To adapt. 2 H VI. II. 4. 68. *v.i.* to associate. V. & A. 689. To be fitting. T. & C. I. 1. 109. Fall out, happen. M.N.D. III. 2. 352.

Souse, *v.t.* to swoop down on, as a falcon.

Sowl, *v.t.* to lug, drag by the ears.

Span-counter, *sb.* boy's game of throwing a counter so as to strike, or rest within a span of, an opponent's counter.

Speed, *sb.* fortune, success.

Speken = speak.

Sperr, *v.t.* to bar.

Spital, *sb.* hospital.

Spital house, *sb.* hospital.

Spleen, *sb.* quick movement. M.N.D. I. 1. 146. Fit of laughter. L.L.L. III. 1. 76.

Spot, *sb.* pattern in embroidery.

Sprag, *adj.* sprack, quick, lively.

Spring, *sb.* a young shoot.

Springhalt, *sb.* a lameness in horses.

Spurs, *sb.* the side roots of a tree.

Squandering, *adj.* roving, random. As II. 7. 57.

Square, *sb.* the embroidery about the bosom of a smock or shift. W.T. IV. 3. 212. Most precious square of sense = the most sensitive part. Lear, I. 1. 74.

Square, *v.i.* to quarrel.

Squash, *sb.* an unripe peascod.

Squier, *sb.* square, rule.

Squiny, *v.i.* to look asquint.

Staggers, *sb.* giddiness, bewilderment. A.W. II. 3. 164. A disease of horses. T. of S. III. 2. 53.

Stale, *sb.* laughing stock, dupe. 3 H VI. III. 3. 260. Decoy. T. of S. III. 1. 90. Stalking-horse. C. of E. II. 1. 101. Prostitute. M.A. II. 2. 24. Horse-urine. A. & C. I. 4. 62.

Stamp, *v.t.* to mark as genuine, give currency to.

Standing, *sb.* duration, continuance. W.T. I. 2. 430. Attitude. Tim. I. 1. 34.

Standing-tuck, *sb.* a rapier standing on end.

Staniel, *sb.* a hawk, the kestrel.

Stare, *v.i.* to stand on end.

State, *sb.* attitude. L.L.L. IV. 3. 183. A chair of state. 1 H IV. II. 4. 390. Estate, fortune. M. of V. III. 2. 258. States (pl.) = persons of high position. John, II. 1. 395.

Statute-caps, *sb.* woollen caps worn by citizens as decreed by the Act of 1571.

Staves, *sb.* shafts of lances.

Stead, *v.t.* to help.

Stead up, *v.t.* to take the place of.

Stelled, *p.p.* fixed. Lucr. 1444. Sonn. XXIV. 1. Starry. Lear, III. 7. 62.

Stickler-like, *adj.* like a stickler, whose duty it was to separate combatants.

Stigmatic, *adj.* marked by deformity.

Stillitory, *sb.* a still.

Stint, *v.i.* to stop, cease. R. & J. I. 3. 48. *v.t.* to check, stop. T. & C. IV. 5. 93.

Stock, *sb.* a dowry. Two G. III. 1. 305. A stocking. Two G. III. 1. 306; 1 H IV. II. 4. 118. A thrust in fencing. M.W.W. II. 3. 24. *v.t.* to put in the stocks. Lear, II. 2. 333.

Stomach, *sb.* courage. 2 H IV. I. 1. 129. Pride. T. of S. V. 2. 177.

Stomaching, *sb.* resentment.

Stone-bow, *sb.* a cross-bow for shooting stones.

Stoop, *sb.* a drinking vessel.

Stricture, *sb.* strictness.

Stride, *v.t.* to overstep.

Stover, *sb.* cattle fodder.

Stuck, *sb.* a thrust in fencing.

Subject, *sb.* subjects, collectively.

Subscribe, *v.i.* to be surety. A.W. III. 6. 84. Yield, submit. 1 H VI. II. 4. 44. *v.t.* to admit, acknowledge. M.A. V. 2. 58.

Subtle, *adj.* deceptively smooth.

Successantly, *adv.* in succession.

Sufferance, *sb.* suffering. M. for M. II. 2. 167. Patience. M. of V. I. 3. 109. Loss. Oth. II. 1. 23. Death penalty. H V. II. 2. 158.

Suggest, *v.t.* to tempt.

Suit, *sb.* service, attendance. M. for M. IV. 4. 19. Out of suits with fortune = out of fortune's service.

Supervise, *sb.* inspection.

Suppliance, *sb.* pastime.

Sur-addition, *sb.* an added title.

Surmount, *v.i.* to surpass, exceed. 1 H VI. V. 3. 191. *v.t.* to surpass. L.L.L. V. 2. 677.

Sur-reined, *p.p.* overridden.

Suspect, *sb.* suspicion.

Swarth, *adj.* black. T.A. II. 3. 71. *sb.* swath. Tw.N. II. 3. 145.

Swoopstake, *adv.* in one sweep, wholesale.

Tag, *sb.* rabble.

Take, *v.t.* to captivate. W.T. IV. 3. 119. Strike. M.W.W. IV. 4. 32. Take refuge in. C. of E. V. 1. 36. Leap over. John,

V. 2. 138. Take in = conquer. A. & C. I. 1 .23. Take out = copy. Oth. III. 3. 296. Take thought = feel grief for. J.C. II. 1. 187. Take up = get on credit. 2 H VI. IV. 7. 125. Reconcile. Tw.N. III. 4. 294. Rebuke. Two G. I. 2. 134.

Tallow-keech, *sb.* a vessel filled with tallow.

Tanling, *sb.* one tanned by the sun. John, IV. 1. 117. Incite. Ham. II. 2. 358.

Tarre, *v.t.* to set on dogs to fight.

Taste, *sb.* trial, proof. *v.t.* to try, prove.

Tawdry-lace, *sb.* a rustic necklace.

Taxation, *sb.* satire, censure. As I. 2. 82. Claim, demand. Tw.N. I. 5. 210.

Teen, *sb.* grief.

Tenable, *adj.* capable of being kept.

Tend, *v.i.* to wait, attend. Ham. I. 3. 83. Be attentive. Tp. I. 1. 6. *v.t.* to tend to, regard. 2 H VI. I. 1. 204. Wait upon. A. & C. II. 2. 212.

Tendance, *sb.* attention. Tim. I. 1. 60. Persons attending. Tim. I. 1. 74.

Tender, *v.t.* to hold dear, regard. R III. I. 1. 44. *sb.* care, regard. 1 H IV. V. 4. 49.

Tender-hefted, *adj.* set in a delicate handle or frame.

Tent, *sb.* probe. T. & C. II. 2. 16. *v.t.* to probe. Ham. II. 2. 608. Cure. Cor. I. 9. 31.

Tercel, *sb.* male goshawk.

Termless, *adj.* not to be described.

Testerned, *p.p.* presented with sixpence.

Testril, *sb.* sixpence.

Tetchy, *adj.* irritable.

Tetter, *sb.* skin erruption. Ham. I. 5. 71. *v.t.* to infect with tetter. Cor. III. 1. 99.

Than = then, Lucr. 1440.

Tharborough, *sb.* third borough, constable.

Thick, *adv.* rapidly, close.

Thirdborough, *sb.* constable.

Thisne, perhaps = in this way. M.N.D. I. 2. 48.

Thoughten, *p.p.* be you thoughten = entertain the thought.

Thrall, *sb.* thraldom, slavery. Pass. P. 266. *adj.* enslaved. V. & A. 837.

Three-man beetle, a rammer operated by three men.

Three-man songmen, three-part glee-singers.

Three-pile, *sb.* the finest kind of velvet.

Three-piled, *adj.* having a thick pile. M. for M. I. 2. 32. Superfine (met.). L.L.L. V. 2. 407.

Tickle, *adj.* unstable. 2 H VI. I. 1. 216. Tickle of the sere, used of lungs readily prompted to laughter; literally hair-triggered. Ham. II. 2. 329.

Ticklish, *adj.* wanton.

Tight, *adj.* swift, deft. A. & C. IV. 4. 15. Water-tight, sound. T. of S. II. 1. 372.

Tightly, *adv.* briskly, smartly.

Time-pleaser, *sb.* time server, one who complies with the times.

Tire, *sb.* headdress. Two G. IV. 4. 187. Furniture. Per II. 2. 21.

Tire, *v.i.* to feed greedily. 3 H VI. I. 1. 269. *v.t.* make to feed greedily. Lucr. 417.

Tisick, *sb.* phthisic, a cough.

Toaze, *v.t.* to draw out, untangle.

Tod, *sb.* Twenty-eight pounds of wool. *v.t.* to yield a tod.

Toged, *adj.* wearing a toga.

Toll, *v.i.* to pay toll. A.W. V. 3. 147. *v.t.* to take toll. John, III. 1. 154.

Touch, *sb.* trait. As V. 4. 27. Dash, spice. R III. IV. 4. 157. Touchstone. R III. IV. 2. 8. Of noble touch = of tried nobility. Cor. IV. 1. 49. Brave touch = fine test of valour. M.N.D. III. 2. 70. Slight hint. H VIII. V. 1. 13. Know no touch = have no skill. R II. I. 3. 165.

Touse, *v.t.* to pull, tear.

Toy, *sb.* trifle, idle fancy, folly.

Tract, *sb.* track, trace. Tim. I. 1. 53. Course. H VIII. I. 1. 40.

Train, *v.t.* to allure, decoy. 1 H VI. I. 3. 25. *sb.* bait, allurement. Mac. IV. 3. 118.

Tranect, *sb.* ferry, a doubtful word.

Translate, *v.t.* to transform.

Trash, *v.t.* lop off branches. Tp. I. 2. 81. Restrain a dog by a trash or strap. Oth. II. 1. 307.

Traverse, *v.i.* to march to the right or left.

Tray-trip, *sb.* a game at dice, which was won by throwing a trey.

Treachors, *sb.* traitors.

Treatise, *sb.* discourse.

Trench, *v.t.* to cut. Two G. III. 2. 7. Divert from its course by digging. H IV. III. 1. 112.

Troll-my-dames, *sb.* the French game of *trou madame*, perhaps akin to bagatelle.

Tropically, *adv.* figuratively.

True-penny, *sb.* an honest fellow. Ham. I. 5. 150.

Try, *sb.* trial, test. Tim. VI. 1. 9. Bring to try = bring a ship as close to the wind as possible.

Tub, *sb.* and tubfast, *sb.* a cure of venereal disease by sweating and fasting.

Tuck, *sb.* rapier.

Tun-dish, *sb.* funnel.

Turk, to turn Turk = to be a renegade. M.A. III. 4. 52. Turk Gregory = Pope Gregory VII. 1 H IV. V. 3. 125.

Twiggen, *adj.* made of twigs or wicker.

Twilled, *adj.* perhaps, covered with sedge or reeds.

Twire, *v.i.* to twinkle.

Umber, *sb.* a brown colour.

Umbered, *p.p.* made brown, darkened.

Umbrage, *sb.* a shadow.

Unaneled, *adj.* not having received extreme unction.

Unbarbed, *adj.* wearing no armour, bare.

Unbated, *adj.* unblunted.

Unbraced, *adj.* unbuttoned.

Uncape, *v.i.* to uncouple, throw off the hounds.

Uncase, *v.i.* to undress.

Unclew, *v.t.* to unwind, undo.

Uncolted, *p.p.* deprived of one's horse. 1 H IV. II. 2. 41.

Uncomprehensive, *adj.* incomprehensible.

Unconfirmed, *adj.* inexperienced.

Undercrest, *v.t.* to wear upon the crest.

Undertaker, *sb.* agent, person responsible to another for something.

Underwrite, *v.t.* to submit to.

Undistinguished, *adj.* not to be seen distinctly, unknowable.

Uneath, *adv.* hardly, with difficulty.

Unfolding, *adj.* unfolding star, the star at whose rising the shepherd lets the sheep out of the fold.

Unhappy, *adj.* mischievous, unlucky.

Unhatched, *p.p.* unhacked. Tw.N. III. 4. 234. Undisclosed. Oth. III. 4. 140.

Unhouseled, *adj.* without having received the sacrament.

Union, *sb.* large pearl.

Unkind, *adj.* unnatural. Lear, I. I. 261. Childless. V. & A. 204.

Unlived, *p.p.* deprived of life.

Unpaved, *adj.* without stones.

Unpinked, *adj.* not pinked, or pierced with eyelet holes.

Unraked, *adj.* not made up for the night.

Unrecuring, *adj.* incurable.

Unrolled, *p.p.* struck off the roll.

Unseeming, *pr.p.* not seeming.

Unseminared, *p.p.* deprived of seed or virility.

Unset, *adj.* unplanted.

Unshunned, *adj.* inevitable.

Unsifted, *adj.* untried, inexperienced.

Unsquared, *adj.* unsuitable.

Unstate, *v.t.* to deprive of dignity.

Untented, *adj.* incurable.

Unthrift, *sb.* prodigal. *adj.* good for nothing.

Untraded, *adj.* unhackneyed.

Unyoke, *v.t.* to put off the yoke, take ease after labour. Ham. V. I. 55. *v.t.* to disjoin. John, III. I. 241.

Up-cast, *sb.* a throw at bowls; perhaps the final throw.

Upshoot, *sb.* decisive shot.

Upspring, *sb.* a bacchanalian dance.

Upstaring, *adj.* standing on end.

Urchin, *sb.* hedgehog. T.A. II. 3. 101. A goblin. M.W.W. IV. 4. 49.

Usance, *sb.* interest.

Use, *sb.* interest. M.A. II. 1. 269. Usage. M. for M. I. 1. 40. In use = in trust. M. of V. IV. 1. 383.

Use, *v.r.* to behave oneself.

Uses, *sb.* manners, usages.

Utis, *sb.* boisterous merriment.

Vade, *v.i.* to fade.

Vail, *sb.* setting (of the sun). T. & C. V. 8. 7. *v.t.* to lower, let fall. 1 H VI. V. 3. 25. *v.i.* to bow. Per. IV. Prol. 29.

Vails, *sb.* a servant's perquisites.

Vain, for vain = to no purpose.

Vantbrace, *sb.* armour for the forearm.

Vast, *adj.* waste, desolate, boundless.

Vaunt-couriers, *sb.* fore-runners.

Vaward, *sb.* vanguard. 1 H VI. I. 1. 132. The first part. M.N.D. IV. 1. 106.

Vegetives, *sb.* plants.

Velvet-guards, *sb.* velvet linings, used metaphorically of those who wear them. 1 H IV. III. 1. 256.

Veney, or venew, *sb.* a fencing bout, a hit.

Venge, *v.t.* to avenge.

Vent, *sb.* discharge. Full of vent = effervescent like wine.

Via, *interj.* away, on!

Vice, *sb.* the buffoon in old morality plays. R III. III. 1. 82. *v.t.* to screw (met.) W.T. I. 2. 415.

Vinewedst, *adj.* mouldy, musty.

Violent, *v.i.* to act violently, rage.

Virginalling, *pr.p.* playing with the fingers as upon the virginals.

Virtuous, *adj.* efficacious, powerful. Oth. III. 4. 110. Essential. M.N.D. III. 2. 367. Virtuous season = benignant influence. M. for M. II. 2. 168.

Vouch, *sb.* testimony, guarantee. 1 H VI. V. 3. 71. *v.i.* to assert, warrant.

Vizard, *sb.* mask.

Waft, *v.t.* to beckon. C. of E. II. 2. 108. To turn. W.T. I. 2. 371.

Wag, *v.i.* and *v.t.* to move, stir. R III. III. 5. 7. To go one's way. M.A. V. 1. 16.

Wage, *v.t.* to stake, risk. 1 H IV. 4. 20. *v.i.* to contend. Lear, II. 4. 210. Wage equal = be on an equality with. A. & C. v. 1. 31.

Wanion, *sb.* with a wanion = with a vengeance.

Wanton, *sb.* one brought up in luxury, an effeminate person. John, V. 1. 70. *v.i.* to dally, play. W.T. II. 1. 18.

Wappened, *p.p.* of doubtful meaning, perhaps worn out, stale.

Ward, *sb.* guardianship. A.W. I. 1. 5. Defence. L.L.L. III. 1. 131. Guard in fencing. 1 H IV. II. 4. 198. Prison, custody. 2 H VI. V. 1. 112. Lock, bolt. Tim. III. 3. 38. *v.t.* to guard. R III. V. 3. 254.

Warden-pies, *sb.* pies made with the warden, a large baking pear.

Warrantize, *sb.* security, warranty.

Warrener, *sb.* keeper of a warren, gamekeeper.

Watch, *sb.* a watch candle that marked the hours.

Watch, *v.t.* to tame by keeping from sleep.

Waters, *sb.* for all waters = ready for anything.

Wealsmen, *sb.* statesmen.

Web and pin. *sb.* cataract of the eye.

Weeding, *sb.* weeds.

Weet, *v.t.* to know.

Welkin, *sb.* the blue, the sky. Tw.N. II. 3. 61. *adj.* sky-blue. W.T. I. 2. 136.

Whiffler, *sb.* one who cleared the way for a procession, carrying the whiffle or staff of his office.

Whist, *adj.* still, hushed.

Whittle, *sb.* a clasp-knife.

Whoobub, *sb.* hubbub.

Widowhood, *sb.* rights as a widow.

Wilderness, *sb.* wildness.

Wimpled, *p.p.* blindfolded. (A wimple was a wrap or handkerchief for the neck.)

Winchester goose, *sb.* a venereal swelling in the groin, the brothels of Southwark being in the jurisdiction of the Bishop of Winchester.

Window-bars, *sb.* lattice-like embroidery worn by women across the breast.

Windring, *adj.* winding.

Wink, *sb.* a closing of the eyes, sleep. Tp. II. 1. 281. *v.i.* to close the eyes, be blind, be in the dark. C. of E. III. 2. 58.

Winter-ground, *v.t.* to protect a plant from frost by bedding it with straw.

Wipe, *sb.* a brand, mark of shame.

Wise-woman, *sb.* a witch.

Witch, *sb.* used of a man also; wizard.

Woman, *v.t.* woman me = make me show my woman's feelings.

Woman-tired, *adj.* henpecked.

Wondered, *p.p.* performing wonders.

Wood, *adj.* mad.

Woodman, *sb.* forester, hunter. M.W.W. V. 5. 27. In a bad sense, a wencher. M. for M. IV. 4. 163.

Woollen, to lie in the = either to lie in the blankets, or to be buried in flannel, as the law in Shakespeare's time prescribed.

Word, *sb.* to be at a word = to be as good as one's word.

Word, *v.t.* to represent. Cym. I. 4. 15. To deceive with words. A. & C. V. 2. 191.

World, *sb.* to go to the world = to be married. A woman of the world = a married woman. A world to see = a marvel to behold.

Wrangler, *sb.* an opponent, a tennis term.

Wreak, *sb.* revenge. T.A. IV. 3. 33. *v.t.* to revenge. T.A. IV. 3. 51.

Wreakful, *adj.* revengeful.

Wrest, *sb.* a tuning-key.

Wring, *v.i.* to writhe.

Write, *v.r.* to describe oneself, claim to be. Writ as little beard = claimed as little beard. A.W. II. 3. 62.

Writhled, *adj.* shrivelled up, wrinkled.

Wry, *v.i.* to swerve.

Yare, *adj.* and *adv.* ready, active, nimble.

Yarely, *adv.* readily, briskly.

Yearn, *v.t.* and *v.i.* to grieve.

Yellows, *sb.* jaundice in horses.

Yerk, *v.t.* to lash out at, strike quickly.

Yest, *sb.* froth, foam.

Yesty, *adj.* foamy, frothy.

Younker, *sb.* a stripling, youngster novice.

Yslaked, *p.p.* brought to rest.

Zany, *sb.* a fool, buffoon.

BIBLIOGRAPHY

Bate, Jonathan, *The Soul of the Age: The Life, Mind and World of William Shakespeare* (Penguin, 2009)

Barber, C. L., *Shakespeare's Festive Comedy* (Princeton UP, 1959)

Billington, Michael, (ed). *Approaches to Twelfth Night* (Nick Hern, 1990)

Bryson, Bill, *Shakespeare* (Harper Collins, 2007)

Leggatt, Alexander (ed), *The Cambridge Companion to Shakespearean Comedy* (Cambridge UP, 2002)

Palmer, D.J. (ed), *Twelfth Night: A Casebook* (Macmillan, 1972)

Penningham, Michael, *Twelfth Night: A User's Guide* (Nick Hern, 2000)

Wells, Stanley (ed), *Shakespeare in the Theatre: An Anthology of Criticism* (Oxford U P., 1997)